TALES FROM THE HORADRIC LIBRARY

Matthew J. Kirby
Tamsyn Muir
Courtney Alameda
Adam Foshko
Barry Lyga
Brian Evenson
Delilah S. Dawson
Catherynne M. Valente

TITAN BOOKS

CONTENTS

INTRODUCTION..7
Written by Justin Parker

THE GOSPEL OF DEATH.........................13
Written by Matthew J. Kirby
Illustrated by Stanton Feng

THE ROSE OF KHANDURAS................33
Written by Tamsyn Muir
Illustrated by Josh Tallman

A COLLAR OF THORNS..........................59
Written by Courtney Alameda
Illustrated by Stanton Feng

THE CARAVAN..83
Written by Adam Foshko
Illustrated by Zoltan Boros

A WHIFF OF SALT...................................105
Written by Barry Lyga
Illustrated by Joseph Lacroix

THE TOMB OF TAL RASHA................129
Written by Brian Evenson
Illustrated by Josh Tallman

WHEN THE DARK SEEPS IN.............147
Written by Delilah S. Dawson
Illustrated by Zoltan Boros

BEYOND THAT DOOR THERE LIES NO LIGHT...163
Written by Catherynne M. Valente
Illustrated by Kelli Hoover

Introduction

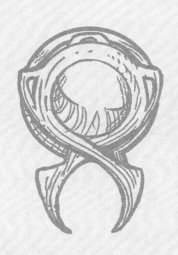

DEAR READER,

In desperate times, we assign the greatest value to that which is of otherwise ordinary import: tools of steel, flame, stone. These things keep us safe through dangerous times, help to fill our bellies, and stave off the darkness for another day.

Yet there is another device we rely on to carry us through, less tangible, perhaps, but no less vital: stories.

Small beacons of light, but essential all the same. Not every story is true, but every story *reveals* truth. Stories look into the teller's heart and tell us not just what our companions know but what they believe—or sometimes what they *want* to believe. When we tell stories—from the most twisted allegories to the plainest texts—we teach, we warn, we enlighten, and occasionally, we entertain and incite.

Such was my goal when, with the blessing of the Horadrim, I first set out on this humble quest to collect stories from the people of Sanctuary.

Long ago, Archangel Tyrael needed the Horadrim to contain the Prime Evils. He gathered the mightiest souls humanity had to offer, a force forged to fight the darkness. When the darkness was contained, they faded into history.

> SMALL BEACONS OF LIGHT, BUT ESSENTIAL ALL THE SAME. NOT EVERY STORY IS TRUE, BUT EVERY STORY *REVEALS* TRUTH.

The new generation of the order—of which I am now a part—was not formed under the guidance of an archangel, but came together in a quest for knowledge. It was scholars, rather than sorcerers or soldiers, who sought to take up the Horadrim's mission. They searched our world to learn and preserve the knowledge of the original order. Force of arms and the arcane are still needed, yes, but now we gather and store the secrets of Sanctuary needed to fight the demons—and sadly, sometimes the angels—who threaten our world.

I am a secret-keeper, a testament-taker, a recorder of myths and prophecies. But my purpose is not only to establish archives that gather the collective knowledge of great scholars and heroes but to preserve the very people of our world who bear witness to its darkest, most trying times. These are the people who do not have ancient spells or high castles to protect them. Like the Horadrim itself, they must rely on their knowledge, knowledge that is shared through their stories.

And now, those stories are shared with you. May this tome help guide your path through our imperiled world.

Mahsati bint Kazmi
HORADRIC LIBRARIAN

The Gospel of Death

MATTHEW J. KIRBY

ILLUSTRATED BY
STANTON FENG

I.

In those days when the Firstborn were still young, there rode a company of four warriors renowned for their strength and cunning as hunters.

There was Corvik, as silent and pale as the clouds and as agile as the wind. Her knives could pierce the toughest of hides to find the soft and inward parts of her prey. There was Bersarik, the strongest of his companions, red of hair and beard, given to merriment when at rest around the cookfire and violent ferocity when roused to anger. There was Helgrotha, black-haired and discerning, who would sometimes let her quarry live to see another sunrise. And lastly, there was Gratian, with warm eyes and dark skin, beloved of the other three for his wisdom and the lethal grace with which he wielded any weapon placed in his hands.

From that company it was said that no animal could conceal its tracks and that no beast could stand against them. Neither the bears and wolves of the forest, nor the great spiders of the fenlands and jungles, nor the cats and worms of the desert dunes. Always the four hunted together, their loyalty as that of kin, their bond as that of blood-sworn, and though they brought swift death upon their blades, they had never known it for themselves. None of the Firstborn in Sanctuary had yet tasted death, for they were still young in those days.

This is how death found them.

One night, Bersarik had a dream, and in his dream he made a spear from a cypress tree and hurled it from the top of a tower in the golden city where he and his companions dwelt. The spear flew high and true, faster and farther than any eagle, over the mountains and into the vast green steppes beyond. When Bersarik awakened, he thought for a time on the meaning of his dream, and then he went to speak of it with the other three.

"A hunt has come into my heart and mind," he said.

Gratian was the first to ask, "Where shall we seek our prey this time?"

"Over the mountains and into the green steppes," Bersarik said, "where we have never hunted."

"And what are we to stalk there?" asked Corvik, her eyes alight with the cold gleam of a deep lake by moonlight.

Bersarik grinned and said, "The wild cattle herds."

This answer gave his companions pause, for the beasts he spoke of were the mighty aurochs of old, now vanished from the land— hunted to extinction, some believe, by the northerners, who wore the aurochs' shaggy coats and grew large and powerful on their flesh. These animals thundered over the steppes, as large as caravan wagons, with broad horns and iron hooves, and their queen was Ahduma the Earthbreaker, she who could thaw the Frozen Sea with the hot breath from her nostrils.

"We have never faced such a challenge," said Gratian. And when Bersarik asked him what he feared, he replied, "Only that we will fail."

To which Bersarik said, "But we are the children of angels and demons. We cannot fail."

They were with him, of course, as he was with them, to the ends and farthest reaches of Sanctuary. And so they prepared themselves for three days, sharpening their weapons and taking strength into their limbs, for once the chase had begun, there would be no rest until they brought their quarry down.

On the fourth day, they left the golden city where they dwelt and traveled northward, until they reached an upland of bare fells, over which a sharp wind howled. Above those shelves they came to the mountains, where gray clouds filled the narrow gorges and gaps with ice, and their crossing was hard. Shrill voices called from the mist around them, hounding them until they entered a high pass, and in that lonely place they were set upon.

Great beasts of the air flew at them from all sides and descended from hidden aeries in the sheer rock walls. The fog made it difficult to see the attackers, but the beat of their wings drove a fetid smell into the mouths and noses of the warriors, and grasping talons tore the air.

In a flash of steel, the four companions drew their weapons and stood shoulder to shoulder facing outward, pushing back their enemy with quick strikes. The flying forms that whipped around them in the mist did not retreat from this sudden defense but simply withdrew to circle them in patient arcs at a distance, more heard than seen as their screeching echoed up and down the pass.

"What are they?" Gratian asked.

"It seems they are kin to blood hawks." Corvik peered at the dark ichor on one of her knives, left by a bite its edge had given. "Though they do not fall as easily."

"Let us test that," Bersarik said, and he threw one of his hatchets at the nearest swooping shadow. The weapon wheeled through the air, landed with a squelch, and the creature dropped as a stone. "There, you see, Corvik?"

he said. "They fall."

"Perhaps," Corvik said, looking upward. "But they are numerous."

Overhead, as if in response to the slaying of their comrade, the voices of the monsters changed from shrieks to a vicious chatter. Their circular paths through the air tightened, and they came closer, emerging from the mist with red eyes, leathery heads, and gray feathered wings as broad as tower shields.

"They are preparing for another assault," Gratian said.

Bersarik growled at that and replied, "Let them come."

When the flying beasts fell upon them, they descended as a winged storm of beak and claw, but the warriors met the attack with their own practiced savagery. Corvik's knives carved meat as easily as air, slicing wing from breast. Gratian's sword sang as it took heads, silencing all within its reach. The point of Helgrotha's spear parted feather, skin, and bone. Bersarik soon cast aside his great axe and went to work with his hands, snatching the birds from the air and rending them asunder in showers of blood.

The skirmish ended quickly, leaving the hard, frozen ground slick with gore, a ring of ruined carcasses around the warriors. The few survivors who had escaped fled back into the mist, up to their nests, their wretched calls fading as the warriors laughed in triumph.

After the battle-fever subsided, the four cleaned their weapons and took many talons as trophies. In doing so, Corvik studied them, noting their curve and the cut of the creatures' beaks, and she said, "They are scavengers."

"Scavengers?" Gratian chuckled at that. "What makes them think they can feast on our flesh as they would the bones of animals?"

"They are mindless," Bersarik said. Then he lifted his head and shouted into the fog, "But we have taught them well!"

Though puzzled by the boldness of their attackers, the hunters were not troubled, for they were the Firstborn, and in those days death had not yet taught them what they would soon learn, and they left that high place to continue their hunt. Some might say they had no need to press on, having found worthy prey there atop the mountains, but they had not yet taken any of their intended quarry, so they went over the pass and came down the other side.

The green steppes stretched beyond the reach of their eyes, a vast expanse of rolling earth that took as much note of them as the endless seas take of a single boat. At first they saw no track or dung of the great aurochs, but they set out undeterred into that land, which was in those days cold and covered in brittle grasses, heath, and gorse. The sun rose three times, and they traveled many leagues before Gratian spotted distant herd-sign.

"I see their trail," he said. When he pointed toward it, his companions scoffed.

> "WHAT MAKES THEM THINK THEY CAN FEAST ON OUR FLESH AS THEY WOULD THE BONES OF ANIMALS?"

"That is no trail," Bersarik said. "It is too big. That is a dry riverbed."

But the hunters learned that Gratian had the right of it when they finally reached the wide track and stood within its ragged borders. The hooves of the aurochs had stamped a furrow in the ground as deep and broad as any channel carved by water or wind, and their teeth had stripped the plain bare, leaving only trampled roots. The four warriors looked around them, dwarfed by the wreckage and beginning to weary, and again Gratian said, "We have never faced such a challenge."

Doubt touched even Bersarik then, but he recalled his dream, and he drew strength from it. "We will prevail. It is our birthright."

The other three believed him. They ignored the weakness creeping into their limbs and followed the herd's trail for another day and night, and in the chill of dawn on their fifth day in the green steppes, they came upon the herd. The aurochs resembled a brown hill on the horizon, and light from the low morning sun blazed through a misty cloud rising off them from their breath and heat. A pale frost covered the ground, and it melted beneath the soles of the warriors' boots, leaving dark footsteps behind them as they crept closer. But before they approached too near the beasts, the hunters dropped to their chests and crawled forward, peering through the grass.

"We'll need to separate one from the herd," Helgrotha said. "That is the only way to bring one of them down."

"Separate it and surround it," Corvik said.

"What of the others?" Gratian asked. "What if they defend their own?"

"Threaten one and the others will run," Bersarik said. "It is the way of herds."

Then they crafted their strategy by choosing their aurochs—one at the edge—and planning their approach. Then they used what contours in the land they could find to weave closer, following the dips and troughs, until they attained their positions. To Corvik fell the task of startling the herd, for she had the greatest skill at stalking unseen and could get closest without being discovered. When she leapt up from the grass, her wailing jolted the aurochs into running unthinking from her. Most of the herd stampeded eastward, while their chosen quarry bolted in the opposite direction. When it came to its senses and realized its mistake, it veered to change its course, but then Helgrotha rose before it from the grass and threw her spear. The shaft landed in the path of the beast and turned it again, even as the herd thundered on. Bersarik and Gratian then closed in, completing the circle, arms outstretched, weapons rattling.

The aurochs was enormous, as tall at its shoulders as Bersarik. It snorted and wheeled, stamping its hooves. It threw its head back, brandishing its wide horns and tossing its shaggy bronze coat. Bersarik roared at it, intending to distract the beast so Gratian could plunge his sword between its ribs to stab its heart, but the ground trembled beneath their feet, and Gratian never struck.

Ahduma the Earthbreaker came then, bellowing with the voice of a thousand trumpets. Fire burned in the aurochs queen's eyes, and smoke poured from her nostrils. Her every hoofbeat shattered the ground as she charged toward the hunters.

Gratian stood between her and the trapped aurochs, and though his companions shouted and pleaded with him to flee, he was too stunned by the bulk of Ahduma's form and ferocity to move. Bersarik threw his great axe at the oncoming beast, but it glanced off one of her horns. He then took up Helgrotha's spear from the ground where it stood, and as he hurled it, he remembered his dream. The spear struck Ahduma in the wedge between her neck and shoulder, a killing blow for a lesser being, but the point could find no purchase in her thick hide and fell away.

As Ahduma reached Gratian, she dropped her head low and lifted him into the air on the tip of her right horn, opening his belly. He fell to the earth tangled with his innards, and then Ahduma barreled over him, utterly breaking him. His companions stood by, powerless, allowing the trapped aurochs to flee, and when it was safely away, Ahduma gave one final snort over Gratian that churned up clods of reddened dirt. Then, satisfied, she also left and returned to her herd.

Bersarik, Helgrotha, and Corvik ran to their beloved, who lay twisted and blinking in the torn earth, unable to voice his agony. His jaw twitched but formed no words, and a few moments later, he died.

II.

In that way, those early days came to an end. Death had found the Firstborn there in the green steppes, though the three hunters did not yet understand it as they knelt around the riven corpse of their companion. They knew only that Gratian was no longer Gratian. Something vital had gone out of him, leaving behind an empty vessel, a cold hearth, a forsaken ruin. Time passed in silence, unreckoned, until the sun had set and dew adorned the fallen brows of the warriors.

Helgrotha was the first to speak. "We are no greater than the lowest beasts that we have hunted and slain. How could we not see? How did we not know? We have been fools."

Corvik agreed. "Even those mindless carrion feeders knew what we did not."

Bersarik said nothing, but he trembled at a battle fought between his heart and mind. In his heart, he wanted to kill Ahduma, but she was mighty, and now he knew fear, for which he hated himself. In his mind, he knew that slaying Ahduma would not bring him peace, for though she had shown the Firstborn they could die, she had not made them mortal. A third truth, he hid from both his heart and his mind.

When the crescent moon rose over the green steppes, Helgrotha shivered under its thin light and looked up. "I must go," she said, and when Corvik asked her where she would go, she answered, "Where death cannot find me."

Corvik doubted that death could be so evaded, for in looking at Gratian's burst flesh she now believed they all carried death hidden somewhere within them, but she kept these thoughts to herself. Helgrotha rose to her feet, and after giving a parting embrace to Corvik and Bersarik, she walked away from them into the darkness.

A short time later, Bersarik said, "I also know what I must do," and when Corvik asked him what he must do, he answered, "I will hold them to account," and when Corvik asked him who he meant, he answered, "Those who made us."

Corvik pondered this and said, "They are more powerful than Ahduma. You will need a powerful weapon to challenge them." Then she took out her knives, and she reached into Gratian with her fingers and her blades. She spread him out across the grass, searching for the secret place where he had carried his death within him, but she did not find it. Defeated in that, she set herself to her next task, fashioning the splayed bones and cords of him into something else. Bersarik watched her work until he could not endure it, thereafter listening with closed eyes to the dull crack of bone and wet slap of tissue, smelling the odors of Gratian's outpouring, awed and confounded, lost in horror, mute and resigned.

When Corvik finished, the pale-yellow weapon she had crafted frightened Bersarik more than Ahduma. It seemed to quiver in his hand, a sword made in hatred for tearing more than slicing, a jagged and thorny branch of bone shards bound together with sinew and uncured strips of hide. Its fragments defied Bersarik's attempts to map where they had come from, as though Corvik had remade Gratian so completely that his original form had been lost, with all his grace and wisdom.

"This weapon is called Severian," Corvik said. "Keep it close to you, and the journey will strengthen it."

Bersarik thanked her and asked what she would do after they parted.

"There are questions I would put to death," she said. "But first, I must find the camp of our hunter."

Bersarik did not know what she meant by that, but neither did he want to know. She stood before him smelling of her labors, her arms stained by the blood of their friend, and he sensed that she had already traveled some distance down a very different road from his. All that remained was to bid her farewell, and then he wrapped Severian in his cloak and strapped the sword to his back.

He set off on a journey that took him from the green steppes over many lands. He crossed treacherous mountains and forded icy rivers, and along the way he spoke to the sword over his shoulder as if it were a companion at his side. He recounted his memories of Gratian, at times with laughter and at times with tears. These words fell on the grain of Severian's hide, softening and weathering it. Then Bersarik voiced his sorrow at Gratian's death, and these words settled into the fibrous web of Severian's ligaments, bracing and tightening them against the pain. Finally, Bersarik hissed his rage and hatred, and these words burned into the pores of Severian's bones, tempering them until they were harder than iron.

> ALONG THE WAY HE SPOKE TO THE SWORD OVER HIS SHOULDER AS IF IT WERE A COMPANION AT HIS SIDE.

Many days and moons passed, and Bersarik suffered many hardships before he came to the dwelling place of the Mother and Father of all, they who had created Sanctuary and the first of the Firstborn. The intricate spires of their fortress-temple rose with angelic grace and precision to such heights that they seemed to touch the cold stars, while its foundations clawed and dug with demonic hunger down to the roots of the world, where the fires of creation could almost warm the stone. It loomed with such terrible grandeur that Bersarik wavered in his resolve at the sight of it, for he had rested little on his journeys and the burden of the knowledge he carried stole much of his strength. But he would not be daunted, and so he pressed ahead toward the house of angels and demons.

Before he attained the first of its many gates, he met one of his kindred on the road. This man, Kalmor, noticed the grime and signs of Bersarik's ordeals and asked him, "Are you well, brother?"

Bersarik answered, "I am well enough for what I must do."

Then Kalmor saw in Bersarik's eyes the dark cast of his heart and mind, and he blocked Bersarik's passage, asking, "What is it you go to do?"

"I go to those who made us," Bersarik said.

Unsatisfied by that answer, Kalmor asked, "For what purpose? What would you say to them?"

And Bersarik answered, "I do not go to speak with them."

Then Kalmor perceived that Bersarik intended violence against their makers, and he resolved to stop Bersarik's blasphemy, by word if he could and by force if he must. "Watch yourself, brother," he said. "Remember it is they who gave us life."

Bersarik laughed, but it was a bitter sound full of poison and treachery. "They gave us *death*," he said, "and they will pay for their sins in kind." Then he demanded that Kalmor let him pass, but having now heard Bersarik's open threat, Kalmor refused.

Neither warrior fully grasped his own peril in that moment, nor did they fully understand the mind and heart of the other, and so their battle began. Bersarik swung his great axe, keeping Severian sheathed for what was to come after, and Kalmor fought with his sword. Their strikes rang out against the walls of the fortress above them and echoed in its courtyards and chambers. As they fought, Kalmor pleaded with Bersarik to lay down his weapon, but Bersarik refused, even though he knew his journey had weakened him and that Kalmor opposed him at full might.

For half a day, they traded blow for blow, blood for blood, neither prevailing, but then Bersarik faltered. His strength had finally begun to wane, and Kalmor succeeded in ripping his great axe from his hand. In desperation, Bersarik drew Severian, but the sword seemed almost to balk in his hand, for it had not been crafted to fight Gratian's own kin, another of the Firstborn. Then Kalmor landed a blow with Bersarik's own axe that clove him from shoulder to breastbone, exposing his beating heart.

The wound shocked both warriors, for never had one of the Firstborn given such injury to another. Bersarik slumped, head bowed, unblinking. Kalmor sat next to him and said, "I am sorry it came to this."

"Do not be," Bersarik said, for as he greeted death, his mind and his heart surrendered their battle to the truth he had hidden from both. "It was I who led our hunt, against Gratian's warnings. I am to blame for his death. In punishing me, you have given him justice." Then, as the blood falling out of him slowed and his heart beat its last, he gasped and said, "You will now see what becomes of me, and you will know what brought me here. Take this bone-sword and use it as you deem best." Then Bersarik died, for death had found Sanctuary, and it could not be stopped.

In that way, Kalmor learned that he also could die—and might have died there had the battle gone a different way. Instead, it was Bersarik who lay split open before him, an affront to life. Kalmor did not know what to do with the corpse, but neither did he welcome the thought of carrion eaters feasting on it, and so he laid the dead warrior in the ground and piled stones over him, to protect him and mark that place. He stood Bersarik's great axe upright in the rocks at the top of the cairn, but he kept the bone-sword as Bersarik had asked. He understood why Bersarik had come, and he shared some of the dead warrior's anger.

After he had finished his grim task, the gate of the fortress-temple opened, and a blazing angelic herald appeared with a summons, saying Kalmor's battle with Bersarik had been observed from on high and a council had been called. Kalmor obeyed the summons and entered that place believing he would be punished for slaying another Firstborn, but when he stood before the council of angel- and demonkind, they did not punish him.

"You fought in our name," they said, and their voices filled Kalmor's mind as a rushing wind and a roaring inferno. "You honored your birthright and legacy."

Kalmor, head bowed before the blinding majesty of the angels and the baleful power of the demons, tightened his grip on Severian and said, "There is more to my birthright than I knew. I have seen it."

"You refer to death," the council said. "But you were never promised a life without end. That gift is not ours to give. We do not even possess it for ourselves. As our children, you will not age, nor will you be touched by the corruptions of plague. But you may die, should your strength be tested by a trial that is beyond you. You may die, should you through carelessness or foolishness place yourself in death's path. Do you understand?"

"I understand now that death is earned," Kalmor said, and then he asked what he should do with Severian.

The demons looked on the bone-sword and said nothing, but the angels turned away from it in disgust, for it reminded them of the weapons and abominations created at the Hellforge. "It is a blasphemy," they said. "Destroy it."

Kalmor bowed his head lower, and the council departed, save one demon who called Kalmor to her.

"What would you have of me, blessed mother?" Kalmor asked.

"Give me that sword," she said.

Kalmor gave Severian to her, and then he

followed her from the council chamber down twisting stairs and along forgotten passages to a place deep in the bowels of the fortress-temple. There she lit a furnace that burned with a heat Kalmor could barely withstand, and he watched as she broke the magic of the bone-sword, melting its greases, unraveling its plaited filaments, and charring its bones. She kept its strength, its pain, and its rage, but she twisted and imprisoned the essence of Severian within a new weapon of her own crafting. The gleaming sword she forged seemed far too broad and too heavy for Kalmor to wield, a blade meant for a much greater being than any of the Firstborn, and yet the demon presented it to Kalmor upon its completion.

"I made this blade for a purpose," she said. "When you are in pursuit of its purpose, the sword will grant you the strength you need to wield it."

"What is its purpose?" he asked.

"Bersarik traveled with others who may share his lust for vengeance," she said. "You will seek them out, and when you find them, you will use this sword to punish them, for in turning against us, they have dishonored their legacy as the Firstborn."

"It will be done, mother," Kalmor said. Then he lifted the sword and discovered that she had spoken the truth. The weapon felt no heavier in his hands than his own, yet it would strike with the devastating might of a demon's blade.

Kalmor left the house of angel- and demonkind with the great sword to pursue his errand, searching across Sanctuary for Corvik and Helgrotha. He explored the uninhabited regions, in the deep shadows beneath silent, towering forests and across the hot, blowing sands of distant deserts. In his travels he witnessed the spreading reach of death's hand, which waited endlessly and patiently for those who earned its embrace. He hunted for many years without any sign or success, and during those days, the Firstborn had children, and their children had children. His journey took him through towns and villages and camps. Everywhere he went, he asked after the two, but none had seen them.

Over time, Kalmor grew disheartened by his failure to fulfill his quest, until one day he came upon a fellow traveler resting beside the road. He shared a meal with her, and when their talk turned to their reasons for being in that place, the traveler said, "I have heard a rumor that might interest you."

"A rumor is better than no word at all," replied Kalmor.

The traveler then told him about a man she had met hastening from a village many days' journey from there, where several had gone missing in a pass through the hills nearby. "The villagers spoke of a great evil that dwells there," the traveler said. "They gave it no name. They said only that its lair is a temple of death." The traveler shivered as if chilled, though she sat in the warmth of the sun. "This man said he would have taken that road had they not warned him, and he believed he had escaped death."

"What do you believe?" Kalmor asked.

"I believe it is often wise to heed rumors," the traveler said. "I would not go near such a place. But if I were seeking an evil that would defy those who made us, I believe it might be found there."

Kalmor thanked the traveler and went in pursuit of this rumor, first to the village, where they begged him to go no farther. They lived and raised their sheep in gray shadows beneath bleak moors, where the wet ground birthed clouds of biting flies and their hearth fires struggled to keep the damp and cold at bay. They promised him that death waited in the pass through the cursed hills.

"Death is earned," he said to them. "But I do not believe this trial is beyond me. I go with a power greater than my own." The sight of the enormous sword he carried kindled hope in some of the villagers, though not in those few who had glimpsed that place for themselves and lived with the memory of it. They all insisted he eat and rest before setting out again. Kalmor obliged them for one night and left them at dawn. The hills he ventured into reminded him of the cairn he had piled over Bersarik many years before. It seemed a sickness festered under their rocky slopes, a withering blight at the roots that sapped and blackened all but the lowest and most wretched scrub attempting to grow there. A suffocating silence lay upon that land, a void where no living thing stirred, and with every step, the absence leeched a hollow in Kalmor's heart.

When at last he heard a sound, it was the screeching of carrion eaters, which only deepened his dread even as it gave him a sign to follow. He looked up to where they circled in the sky, and he moved toward them, knowing death would be found close by.

That is how Kalmor found Corvik and the temple she had built. The sight of her lair almost caused him to quake, and he doubted whether even the sword he had been given could stand against such an obscenity. He stepped onto a causeway paved with the skulls of animals and Firstborn that climbed upward flanked by impaled, eviscerated corpses. The dead faced toward the temple, arms outstretched and draped with the coils of their own viscera, and as Kalmor walked that harrowing road, he had to shut his ears against the sound of moaning for fear it was not the voice of the wind he heard.

At the top of the causeway stood an oratory constructed of flesh and bone, and Kalmor could not begin to count or measure the number of dead required to build it. The alchemy of desiccation and putrefaction had rendered its raw materials into a congealed mass of tissue that oozed and wept from vivid fissures, and from which hair still sprouted here and there. Kalmor thought the smell of it could drive him mad as he marched toward it, eyes and nose burning.

The door to the temple gaped like a chapped mouth, and before Kalmor entered it, he drew the sword he had been given. Its power filled him, as though the weapon sensed where it was and was eager to begin the work for which it had been forged. He stepped inside and heard a voice with the fluid warmth of fresh blood.

"Have you come to die for me?" Corvik asked.

She stood behind an altar that was swathed in a skirt of thick, waxen runnels of dried

blood and untold layers of suffering. Upon the altar lay the gutted body of an old man, organs still wet and quivering, creased mouth and eyes open wide and unmoving.

"I have been sent to punish you," Kalmor said.

Corvik stepped out from behind the altar and came toward him, all of her once-pallid skin now turned a mottled red. "Who has sent you to punish me?" she asked.

"Those who made you," Kalmor replied.

Her frown seemed almost disappointed as she said, "I do not fear them, and neither should you. There is a power far greater than theirs."

"You speak of death," Kalmor said.

She nodded and said, "It is the only power that matters. It is the power I have sought and worshipped these many years. It is the power I will master, and then I will rule over even those who made us."

Kalmor looked around them at her monstrous desecration and said, "You did not do this to master death. You did this to master your fear of death, and now that your death is here, I wonder if you are afraid."

Corvik leapt at him with a speed far beyond what he expected, and her knives slashed at him with startling strength. The essence of all the dead that she had claimed filled her with scavenged power, and she drove Kalmor from her temple, out onto the causeway, shouting, "I have witnessed death in all its shapes, methods, and guises. I have looked into its eyes and tasted living flesh. It is you who stinks of fear."

Though Kalmor was indeed afraid, he shouted back at her, "I will slay you as I slew Bersarik!"

At which she suddenly halted her attack, laughing at him, and said, "You lie."

"I watched the last beat of his heart," Kalmor said.

Corvik held up her knives and readied herself to end him as she said, "Then tell me what became of Bersarik's weapon, if you truly slew him."

Kalmor raised the demon-forged blade and said, "It was remade."

Corvik looked closely at the great sword and descried the truth of its lineage, whereupon she lowered her knives under the weight of nearly forgotten memories and whispered, "Gratian?"

Kalmor swung the blade. It passed through Corvik's arm, taking her hand, and stopped deep in her side, almost cutting her in two. She folded apart and spilled onto the causeway, and as she lay there, tears washed some of the dark stain from under her eyes.

"I am afraid," she said, and died.

Kalmor stood over her, surrounded by the silent howling of the dead, and could find no pity in his heart for her. "You earned this," he said, and he left her body out in the open for the carrion eaters that had guided him there, who perhaps still knew more of death than she.

He did not stop in the village. They would have asked what he had seen and done, and he did not want to speak of those things, but they witnessed his safe return down the road. In that way, they knew the trial had not been beyond him, though the pass through the hills remained a haunted place for many generations after, avoided by all save the foolish and those drawn to evil.

For many more years, Kalmor wandered in search of Helgrotha, the last of Bersarik's companions, and for years she eluded him. Though the Firstborn continued to grow and prosper in Sanctuary, Kalmor again became discouraged. The great sword he carried felt heavier in his hand, as though it knew of his failure and had begun to revoke the strength it had lent him. He did not blame the weapon for this, and he told it as much one night as he sat before his cookfire.

"Perhaps she is already dead," he said. "If she moves under the sun, I would have found her." The sword replied only with a dark glint that put Kalmor in mind of the midnight sky above him. "Perhaps she does not move under the sun," he said, and from that moment he searched for Helgrotha after the sun had set.

His wanderings acquainted him with the creatures of the night and the many depths of shadow cast by moonlight. His search took him down strange roads and hidden turnings until one evening he came to a great woodland. He saw no road into it, nor even a footpath, and he felt many threatening eyes upon him. He went to a nearby inn and inquired of the folk there to learn more about the wood, but he found that none would speak of it, and the very mention of it seemed to dim the light of the candles. Then a hunter arrived, and Kalmor was told he should speak with that man if he would know about the wood, so Kalmor asked him.

"Only a fool would go in there," the hunter said, and when Kalmor asked whether he went in, the hunter replied, "I do, and I am counted a fool. But I am not a fool. I go in only when the sun is high, and I leave before it sets."

"What happens after the sun has set?" Kalmor asked.

The hunter leaned in close to murmur, "At night, that place is the domain of the Wood Witch. She knows every branch on every tree, and she can speak with the animals, and they do her bidding. Many a snare of mine has been robbed of its bait without springing. Many a time have I caught some creature watching me with eyes that know too much. The Wood Witch has taught them well."

> "YOU DID THIS TO MASTER YOUR FEAR OF DEATH, AND NOW THAT YOUR DEATH IS HERE, I WONDER IF YOU ARE AFRAID."

Kalmor thanked the hunter and waited at the inn for daylight. Then he went back to the wood, and from his first step under the trees, he felt the awareness of countless, nameless things and breathed air that was thick and laden with malice. He worked his way inward, pressing through bramble and ducking beneath the heavy, low branches of colossal trees, until he reached a glade. At its center rose a tall standing stone, and the silent dignity of it demanded reverence. It reminded Kalmor of the cairn he had raised over Bersarik, and he sat down next to it to wait.

When night fell over the wood, the glade and standing stone glowed with thin brilliance in the light of the moon and stars. Kalmor stood and raised his voice, shouting Helgrotha's name. His summons sounded weak in that place, as though even the trees ignored him, but he called again, and then a third time.

In answer, the wood sent a fox that circled Kalmor and the standing stone at a distance, its tail flashing in the tall, soft grass. When the animal returned to the edge of the clearing, it paused to stare at Kalmor before vanishing. Then the wood sent a great spider that did not come into the moonlight. It skittered and clicked from the trees, circling the glade, studying Kalmor with many glittering eyes, and when it departed, it left silken nets behind in the high branches. Then the wood sent an owl with lustrous silver plumage and onyx talons. It swooped and circled high above Kalmor, and it screeched at him before it soared away. Then the wood sent an enormous bear, which did not circle the glade. It charged at Kalmor from the trees so quickly that he had not even raised his blade when he felt himself tumbling through the air, heaved aloft by a single swipe of the beast's paw.

Kalmor landed in the soft grass without breath and without his weapon, gasping as the bear came again, brown coat rippling, white teeth gleaming. Kalmor believed that maw would tear out his throat in the next moment, but a calm voice floated through the clearing.

"Bersarik, halt," Helgrotha said, and the bear obeyed.

She carried a spear, and a short sword hung from her belt. Kalmor looked for his own blade and found where it had fallen several paces away, well out of his reach and blocked by the immensity of the bear. Helgrotha stood next to the animal and laid a hand against its shoulder.

"This is no common hunter," she said. "Let us learn something of him before you eat him."

Kalmor staggered to his feet and said, "I knew Bersarik. Do you call this bear by that name to honor its namesake?"

Helgrotha shook her head and answered, "I mourn its namesake still."

That softened Kalmor's heart toward her as he spoke, saying, "You are Helgrotha," which she acknowledged, and when she asked his name, Kalmor gave it. "You should know that I slew Bersarik, and I slew Corvik," he said.

Helgrotha showed no surprise at this. She merely sighed and said, "Now you have come to kill me, and I see you have been given the means to do it. I suppose I have been waiting for you all these long years. I gave up living under the sun and moved only under cover of night, trying to hide from death. Still death has found me, and still I am a fool."

"How are you a fool?" Kalmor asked.

She pondered her answer and then gave it, saying, "I see now that I cannot hide from death. No one can, nor can death be mastered through worship and flattery. To rage in defiance of death is to hasten it."

Kalmor agreed with her and said, "Death is earned."

Helgrotha shook her head, and stroking the bear's fur, she said, "All my years of hunting and all my years of hiding have taught me that death simply is, and that it must be. What is a fortress without a wall? What is a glade without the forest? It is the border that defines the worth and meaning of what lies within it, and death is but the inevitable boundary of life."

Kalmor disagreed with her. He still believed mortality to be weakness, a disease the Firstborn had been spared, and for that he felt they should be grateful, but he kept these things to himself. Helgrotha's lack of gratitude offended him, but he knew she carried no blasphemy in her heart, nor a lust for vengeance against those who had made them. So when she asked him when he intended to kill her, he answered, "I do not intend to kill you. My errand is finished."

He walked around the bear to where the great sword lay, its purpose fulfilled. When he bent to pick it up, he found it almost too heavy to lift, but with effort he raised it over his head. He then brought the blade down flat against the standing stone, and the metal sparked against the rock with a peal of thunder and a rushing wind. The weapon broke in two, and Kalmor buried the pieces there in the glade.

> "I SEE NOW THAT I CANNOT HIDE FROM DEATH. NO ONE CAN, NOR CAN DEATH BE MASTERED THROUGH WORSHIP AND FLATTERY."

Helgrotha watched his task with sadness at the final ending of her former company.

Then Kalmor looked again at the giant bear and said to Helgrotha, "I will leave your wood now, if I may go in peace."

"You may leave as you wish, unharmed," she replied. "But peace you must find for yourself."

Then Kalmor and Helgrotha parted, he to his fate and she to hers. There are many stories told of what they each did after their meeting, and how they both came finally to their deaths, but those are tales told elsewhere.

The Rose of Khanduras

TAMSYN MUIR

ILLUSTRATED BY
JOSH TALLMAN

As I write this testimony, I understand that in all likelihood I ought to be hanged for it, and not for nothing. I am as guilty as sin in this matter. I won't attempt to defend myself or persuade anyone I was innocent, because nobody would believe it, and because I wasn't. How I loved her!—in what agonies I feared her, and feared for her!—how contemptible she was, that miserable creature who even now folk call the "Countess," she who believes herself the Rose of Khanduras!

But she was my mistress and deep in my bones remains my mistress still, to the end of her days and mine, whatever other name she has stolen for herself: and these guilty days of my own will surely end soon. I am not certain to live after what comes next. If I am to defend myself, I will say only that I was a girl, and that my mistress was not just as beautiful as everyone said, but more so. Once upon a time, that monstrous Countess was the loveliest creature anyone ever laid eyes upon; but to me, she was just as willful and pig-ignorant and miserable a child who ever grew up in the fens.

I.

Now you may say that I am a coward. But no cowards grew up in the marshes, and it was a hard life, even before all that happened. If you who read this are not familiar with the Khanduras marshes and the lands here, I must first explain them, because they also explain the Countess.

The lands she inherited were vast and poor. Her family were the only nobles and had no neighbors of the same status as themselves, only their villeins and crofters, which left them the surviving lords of a blighted landscape.

There were once many castles in the land, but they had fallen to ruin, absorbed by the trees and the earth itself, though many of their dark roots were left underground. The crofters got very little good out of that sticky, muddy, icy soil. Most people made charcoal. We sold it onward in great carts, and I hear that it got sent to Ivgorod and as far as Lut Gholein, though we were paid but poor coin for it. There was oil coming out of fissures in the ground, what they call swamp oil, and some poor creatures would soak it up in woolly blankets and send it on to a monastery to make medicines with. Nobody was rich in the marsh, but there was a pride there, that we could live in our own fashion where the nesh of the south feared to go—and men and women could make a bit of money off them, too, leading travelers safely through the bogs and dangers—and if you will believe me, we were terribly proud of the noble family, and of the girl there too. How little she needed our pride, when she had so much of her own! But we were proud of her, as you would be proud of a captured tiger . . . as you would be proud of a scar.

Their keep was falling into disrepair even then. We called it the Big House, as a fen joke. It must have been a stout stone fortress once, but the moat had turned to sludge, and the bailey all round it couldn't keep a cat out. The family were obliged to live in its northmost tower, which had survived best out of the rest of the keep. It was whispered that there was fabulous wealth hidden in the Big House's coffers, trinkets and jewels aplenty with coins hidden in the rafters, but none of this showed in the upkeep of the lands and house. We all took it for a fairy story.

It was inarguable that the family was of strong noble blood, some of the nicest in Khanduras, or had been, a long time ago. They found it hard to get wives and husbands in the swamp, or anywhere else. Certainly they had been reavers of people if not of gold and gems. When I was a child, my granfer told me that they used to practice bride-theft and groom-theft, carrying off poor young men and women forcibly on horseback. I could believe it of the family: one wouldn't put anything past them, only they were all so particular. I find it easier to believe that they married themselves and their kin and cousins just to keep that precious blood among themselves. There was a great family crest hanging over their fireplace in terribly old-fashioned writing I could hardly make out, but the mistress liked to read it to me: "By the Blood of my Hart," with a ghastly preserved head of a stag, some of the skin off and much of the skull showing. The mistress once condescended to explain to me the jest, but all I could see was that the family cared very little for the hart, or for the heart either, and only thought about the blood.

Oh, and she was the worst of them! At the tender age of just sixteen, she was the very worst. I came to her when I was but two years her elder, but I seemed both a century older and yet a swaddling babe. She was old in her depravity then, and young in her ignorance. I was very pretty for what I was, and for what I cared, for beauty in the swamp is considered a snare and a foxlight. I was cured of preening as a child by my granfer saying, "The brightly colored petals are the poison." I think he was thinking of my mother, his son's wife. She had

> I CAME TO HER WHEN I WAS BUT TWO YEARS HER ELDER, BUT I SEEMED BOTH A CENTURY OLDER AND YET A SWADDLING BABE.

been some very distant cousin of the family itself, had served as some degraded manner of lady-in-waiting to my mistress's mother and been suckled at the same wet nurse. She had education, which was why I could write and figure, but she fell in love with my father, who was just a blacksmith. She did not darken the doors of the keep after that, but lived in the swamps—and died in the swamps, too, a few years before I went to serve the mistress, and my father died a year after, as he had no interest in living. Even in life he cared more for my mother than for the forge, or for me, or for anyone. I was an industrious little body, and I kept the house and oiled the tools as my parents mooned over each other. I had more of my grandmother than my mother in me. My granfer loved me but hated her. But that's my own history, and of no consequence except that I was pretty, not pallid like the other swamp girls but with roses in my cheeks—always strong as a little horse—and that I was not just crofters' stock, but noble blood ran through my veins. Otherwise, the mistress never would have suffered me.

There was nobody in that Big House to look after her. Her mother had died in the birthing of her; her father was obsessed with book learning of the most religious kind, half a hermit already, and had surrounded himself with cheese-faced priests and monks and even let them squat inside the house. I think they were always hoping that they would see some of that fabled money for themselves if they waited long enough. They lived inside the old chapel and gave a service once a year that all us swamp folk dutifully attended, on the false belief that an unwanted meal for free had some virtue in it that the same meal for money wouldn't. Otherwise, there were grandams and cousins of six different sorts for her, but loners they were all to a body, and odd, too, and fearful to look at; she wanted none of them. They got a wet nurse for her, but packed her off again pretty quick once the babe was weaned. Men said later she was born with a full set of teeth and ripped at the nurse's breast when first it was given her, but that's a silly falsehood. I knew the woman myself, and a weak, slack-wristed body she was, unfit to give a dog suck in my opinion, let alone my mistress. After the wet nurse, they ran through two women a year trying to find someone to care for the girl, for she tired of them all and made their lives unbearable, so that they would not and could not stay. No tutor could teach her. No lady could make her pluck out a tune on the viol or interest her in acting the chatelaine. She could ride a horse, and that was all. And so the babe grew into a girl, who grew into a woman—beastly—untaught—as unbroken and maddened as a rabid dog . . . but as lovely to look on as a new morning.

That was how she was when I met her, as I said. She was sixteen, and I was nearly nineteen. She took a fancy for my looks one day when she was out and about among the crofters, on a horse she hadn't grown tired of yet. I had gone closer to the Big House than usual on some errand, and she had seen me. Didn't know me from a blade of grass, of course, but that was always her way and her caprice. When my granfer came to me saying that I was wanted at the Big House, I laughed in his face.

"I'm not interested in playing nanny goat to that young hellion," I said, "and I'm not suited to it, for all that everyone else they've got in to do it has been a great deal worse." And I wouldn't say *yea* to his pleas, nor to my neighbors, for all they begged that I not bring the wrath of the Big House down on them. A man came down every day for a sennight— cozening or begging or threatening—until at last, she came down herself, horse and all. One day I looked up to see her standing on my threshold.

She took my breath away, half with the flaming cheek of the thing, half with admiring her. She had skin like the petals of a flower and just as delicately tinted: too pale for beauty by village standards, most of the time, but right then she had roses enough. She had been riding hard and was blazing with anger. Her long hair was coming free from pins she had stuck indolently up in it, for she had nobody to care for her hair and was too proud and lazy to fend for herself: hair so lightly and gently fair that it was snow-gold, white nearly, and Nature had played that charming trick it sometimes plays on blondes by giving her dark eyes—brilliant, velvety brown eyes, to set off that hair and that skin. She was holding the whip of her horse, and she cried out to me—

"How dare you not come when I want you? You *will* come, I say."

"I say I won't, so it's your will against mine," I told her, keeping my temper. "I'm bigger than you by a head, stronger in the arms, and I could certainly throw you back through that door if I had a mind to it. What now, my lady?"

How she gawped! Yet I had made her think, and she could see I wasn't to be cowed either; she had a ferocious, petty temper, but she was not a fool. She fondled her whip with a sort of red spark in those pretty brown eyes, as though she wanted badly to use it on me, and looked at me with a kind of terrible hunger as though I were a meal. She always was like that, with anything she thought worth the looking at; she could look at a sunset with tears of fury standing in her eyes that she couldn't possess it.

"They'll pay you," she said shortly. "The terms aren't hard. You must be my companion— and dress me and fetch my bath and do things for me. You carry yourself nicely. You hold your head far better than the other common people. Get your things and come. No . . . don't bother with your things. I won't have piggish peasant furze and fustian around me. Peasant things make me sick."

This did not make me love her any more. "I don't want for money," I said. "We have enough, which is more than many can say, and if we didn't, I'd go elsewhere, for I'm not afraid of work. Why should I go with you? Because of your beauty? You won't be beautiful in the grave, my lady."

I was goading her, and I thought she would strike me; but she smiled. I never could bring her to believe that her beauty might fade. "You don't look much older than I am," she said, "but you talk like an old woman. It amuses me. I've decided. You'll come home with me."

Before I could say a word to this extraordinary speech, she strode up to me and seized one of my hands. I let her. When she saw that it was work-chapped and red from lye and laundry, she pushed my hand roughly away from herself, and she changed color. The roses in her cheeks went dead, and she looked like a corpse. She was honestly frightened. "You're ruining all your beauty," she cried. "They've made a peasant of you. Your hands are ugly." And she seemed so panicked that I thought she would faint dead away.

Ah, but this is what touched me—not her silly speechifying about ugly hands or peasantry, but the strangeness of her. She sat down on a stool there and then in my rude cottage as though she had been taken ill. I knelt before her and said, "Don't fratch so. There's nothing to fret yourself about," until she breathed hard, in and out, and eventually some of that blush tint came back into her cheeks.

She stared at me—*through* me, rather—and she said:

"They say you have the Blood." (She meant I was a connection of the family, of course, but she always put things in that strange way, even back then.) "Yet you don't look it. Your hair is too dark, though it curls nicely. Your eyes are the wrong color; blue eyes are weak eyes, though that dark blue isn't as bad as some. And your nose is too small. Yet you're beautiful . . . It's because of the Blood, of course. Nobody baseborn can ever be truly beautiful."

No girl alive fancies aspersions made on her nose, nor her home people either; but I felt impatient with her, not angry, for she wasn't being what I would call sensible. I said, "And yet there are those living up at the Big House who are ugly as sin, for all they have is this so-called Blood. How do you explain that, my lady?"

"I can't," she said simply. "I need you to explain it to me."

And so I was caught like a bird in a snare. I did not give a fig for being "wanted," but "needed" was another matter; my vanity was never flattered by references to my hair curling, but it was easily touched by the idea that I had something of interest to say. I said, warningly, "At the end of the spring, I'll leave if I don't suit," and all she said was—

"You'll stay forever."

Forever! As it was, I nearly didn't stay those first few weeks in that great, dreary tower, which was less snug than the rudest mud hut of the poorest crofter. My mistress had a great stone room with lofty beams, and I slept in a bed close to the fire in the same room. The servants would never have lit a fire for me if I slept alone; they'd as soon not have lit one for *her*, only they all went in living terror of her. I saw her slap the boy who came to stoke the hearth, all because she didn't like the look of him, and box the ears of the cook's girl with the breakfast, calling her slovenly. So I brought her breakfast, to spare the ears of the cook's girl, and fixed something of her dress when the fire was being seen to, to spare the boy. How she saw these things, and how she laughed! We quarreled; I told her she was spoiled and cruel and a great many things besides, but she simply drank it up like wine. At the end of the second sennight, I really harmed her by saying she wasn't to wear some trifling ornament or another. She could dress in awful taste—a dreadful thirst for rich colors—but the first time I told her so, she turned white, then liver-colored; then she made to strike me.

But I grasped that delicate hand, then the other. And when she struggled, I told her to hold, that she would bruise her own wrists, and that I meant them to be black-and-blue if she persisted. Her face was purple with fury and hurt pride. I understand now what I did not understand then: how much I had hurt her by ever suggesting she could be anything less than beautiful or ladylike or tasteful. She had always thought she intuitively knew everything from being noble, like a bird building a nest or a beast bringing down prey. She kept saying, "I'll kill you! I'll kill you! I won't have you near me," and grew all the more wild when I laughed at her.

"Then I'll leave tomorrow—and you won't be any prettier in bright orange when I do," said I.

"You envy me! You're spiteful," she gasped. "You great, clumsy peasant girl—I'll kill you! Oh, how I'll make you suffer!"

She worked herself up into such hysterics that I slapped her. I slapped her a deal lighter than she'd slapped the hearth boy, but she dropped as though I'd slashed her throat. I bundled her into a chair and bathed the reddened cheek with cold water, and I undid the dreadful orange stomacher that did her no favors (nor would it have done favors to any fair-haired beauty) and gave her rose color instead, and smoothed her locks. She stared dully at herself in the mirror as I worked, mumbling frightful threats, until I said—

> I SLAPPED HER A DEAL
> LIGHTER THAN SHE'D
> SLAPPED THE HEARTH
> BOY, BUT SHE DROPPED
> AS THOUGH I'D SLASHED
> HER THROAT.

"There: as lovely as a goddess born. You've got eyes; see for yourself."

She stared at the vision of her face in the mirror and then started to laugh—a high, strange, unearthly laugh. Impulsively, she took my hand and said: "You strange creature. I don't understand you. I knew you wouldn't be like the others." And she laughed again, that curious little laugh, and kept looking at herself with her big dark eyes and pressed my hand to her soft cheek.

"Must I pack my things now?" I said.

"Not on your life," she said imperiously. "You serve me, and only me."

Ah, for that was how she mastered me! I would bluster and act an old woman and nag and scold, for I think she rather enjoyed this maternal playacting: even liked me to prose about her behavior and call her beastly, as she turned that flowerlike face to me in wonderment. Nobody had ever cared to criticize her before, and she listened to my criticisms as though I were some exotic bird she was keeping, trilling for her entertainment. I thought at one time I was educating her—but I know better now.

She liked me to braid her hair. So help me, I was as invested now in her beauty as she was, and she could tell it; I loved neatness and beauty and harmony, and it was under my hands that she became elegant and looked cared-for and less wild. She knew that if I said something didn't become her, I meant it, and if I wanted her to lie down and stop raging because it would ruin her complexion, why then I meant that too. I even got her to stop slapping the hearth boy because I had started taking proper care of her nails and didn't want my work to be for naught. But the rod was never truly in my hand, if only I had not been so blind to see it. Every time she softened, every time she caught my hand up and looked at me with her great velvety eyes, a little mocking even in solemnity, and said—"Oh, Nan! My quibbling nanny goat, know your mistress"—oh, I was mastered then; just a woman's maid, with not a tongue in her head for reprisal or reproof.

That was how I knew she was coaxing me: "Nan," "sweet Nan," "dear Nan," not the mocking "Nanny" or "Nanny goat"; not my own real birth name, for she used it barely more than I use it in this document. And I called her very properly "Mistress," though she knew the difference between me saying it for propriety and meaning it. And there were many times when she meant that she should be "Mistress" for me, like I was a priest at her altar. But I did not think I cared—I was the only one in that great damp wreck of a place who could make her mind me. I loathed the others, and I was told more than once by an uncle of hers that I would be out on my ear if I wasn't the only one who could make that vixen come to heel; when I told my mistress that, her eyes went black. He had a terrible accident soon after, for his saddle strap was slit and came off, and he broke part of his back in the fall; my mistress was so unmoved and uninterested I hardly dared think she had any part in it.

As for her—whose name I never say—when I was very moved, I called her pet names like "Daisy" or "Lily," wildflowers, common weeds, for she loathed the things: I thought it would teach her that beauty was not just found in fine seeds and hothouses; but the most she ever did was laugh a little sometimes, at *Daisy*. She knew I could teach her nothing. I would have walked days in the swamp with bare feet, not bothering to pluck the leeches from my skin, to gather her a blade of grass that she wanted, to hear my mistress say, *Oh, darling Nan*. It is always like this with those who believe they are strong, but aren't.

It was like that between us, maid and mistress, after two years. My mistress had learned that I knew which colors were most fit for her, and how best to style her hair for an effect, and—perhaps—how to keep her temper when there were others around; or how to let her temper out only on those whom I could deal with for her. After two years, she was more beautiful than ever and more terribly aware of that blood running through her veins. The crofters said she was the loveliest creature to ever walk the earth, and even those travelers who came to the Big House—from the Marches, and from beyond the monastery—said they had never seen a woman more beautiful, whose features were more perfect, with eyes more speaking and alluring.

Her family were furious with her, for sometimes young men, and older men who should have known better, came to see her. She flirted with them, spoke slightingly to them, and in the end ignored them: and how she and I laughed, alone in her tower room, when they walked off into the marsh with the look of men like to die! I should have been more sympathetic, but they were such fools. Sometimes she turned down men of real noble blood, arguably *better* blood than ran in her veins, and certainly with a weight of coin in their coffers that many'd find better than blood... but she shook her head at all of them.

"Baseborn," she would call one man with lands and properties that stretched the Sweetwater; "Bird faced," another, with a family lineage that went back eight hundred years. She said to me, decidedly, "If their blood was truly good, then they would be beautiful—they would attract me. They don't, so it can't." At one point, I thought her aunts and uncles and the priests would all join together and beat her into submission. But I stood by her, stood like a guard dog before her door and savaged all comers. I thought she would take nobody, and I warned her she might come to regret it—like a field mouse taking nothing into his hoard, in hope of the finest corn, only to starve in winter. She would toss her long hair, smoothed by my hand and my brush, and laugh with a sound like a rippling stream.

I confess I thought nobody handsome enough for her, though I prayed that a king might come through, as it seemed she would hardly take anyone less.

II.

It was then that the Comtessa and her people came to the keep.

This will be an ugly part of my confession, but I must write it all. I still don't know who the Comtessa is, was, or *what* she was, which is perhaps the better question. I cannot even write down her full name, for when she was announced to us, her and her whole riotous throng of followers and courtiers and parasites, it was much too long and grand to remember.

They came in the dark of the night and knocked boldly at the castle door. From the stairs, all I could see were their horses—horses beyond count, and firelight flickering on their jewels and doublets and feathers—a motley and fearful crew, I thought. I did not like them. What kind of people travel uncloaked in autumn, with their horses steaming from cold, without a red nose or ague among them? Who rides through the swamp in the dark, on a moonless night? But the whole family, despite being roused from their beds, were enchanted by such extravagance—blinded by how richly they dressed for travelers, as though they had no fear of bandits or violence.

I took less note of the lustrousness of their cloaks than I did of how youthful they all

were—not a graybeard in the company—how strangely alike they were in their beauty: for even the least of them was handsome, and the greatest of them was the Comtessa.

The Comtessa threw all her lovely followers into the shade. She was tall for a woman, strapping tall, with dead-black hair I would soon learn fell straight to her ankles if she unbraided it; black hair with no lights in it, and brown skin like silk. I had never seen a complexion so perfect except in my lady's face. Certainly I had never seen anyone, not even my mistress, girt for travel in silk and velvet and lace—all dyed so deep a red they were nearly purple—as though such rich stuffs could be discarded with a thought. She spoke with a musical accent I was too ignorant to guess at.

All of that retinue called her "Comtessa," and some foreign title in their own tongue: and I know not now if she came east of the Tamoe, or farther on and a Kehjistani, or from the regions of Teganze, or a royal beauty from the steppes, or if she emerged out of the barbaric north. She was always vague, and my mistress never cared for either history or geography. All I know is that I had never seen a rival for my mistress's beauty, and that I was fearful in that moment of how my mistress might panic at being so matched.

The Comtessa's retinue were traveling through Khanduras on pilgrimage, she said, though I never believed it. She did not seem the type to throw coins to monks and pray at shrines. She came to ask permission of the house to rest there, though her eyes lingered on my mistress when she said it. The priests and family began to posture, to bleat about room and board, but my mistress came forward fearlessly. I regretted her looking so exceptionally fine that night, in soft blue, with her pale hair bound high on her lovely head; but she looked irresistible, and I had done it with my own hands.

"Have you heard of me?" my mistress demanded coldly of the Comtessa.

The Comtessa took my mistress's hand in hers, the picture of sophistication. She had a huge jewel glimmering on one finger, a ruby the size of a pigeon's egg.

"I heard there was a girl here of uncommon beauty," she said. "Now I know I never heard of you at all. To call you 'beautiful' is to contemplate the poverty of language as we know it. I know of no word for you in any language fit for your face." And she kissed my mistress on the hand and both cheeks, in the elegant way of Caldeum.

My mistress's face changed. I had feared she would despise this beautiful stranger; now I could see she was drinking in the vision of her, the satins and silks, the expensive dyes, the perfection of form, as though all these things were wine. Her mouth softened. I had never seen her look so lovely.

"I think you speak well and truly, Comtessa," said my incorrigible mistress.

The Comtessa threw back her shapely head and laughed.

"To have met a creature so comprehending of her charms," she said, "is almost as good as the sight of your face. Pah! to false modesty, to the milk-and-water misses of this place. They had no blood in their veins, but I see *you* do.

Give me succor, my lady. Give me beds for my people, and let me rest here at this shrine, heretofore unknown—for *you* are the greatest miracle of my pilgrimage so far."

She needn't have laid it on so thick, for my lady wouldn't have had the faintest clue of how to spell or figure *succor*, but my mistress blushed until her dark eyes glowed. She immediately played at chatelaine and demanded rooms for all the company, bossed the servants, and cried for the horses to be fed and watered. She would have fed the travelers too, though the gods only knew on what, but the Comtessa said they had fed enough and could hunt for game on the morrow. The priests breathed a devout sigh of relief; and I did my mistress's bidding—set off on the excited orders she set me, to make these people comfortable—never liking it for a moment. The company smiled too much, never showing their teeth, and walked too softly. But my mistress, excited as a child, was full of their charms: their health and beauty, their silks and figured velvets, their fashions. She was full of the ruby as big as a pigeon's egg, and for one indulgent moment I saw in her an excitable child at a feast, gloating over rich clothes. But then she said—

"But the Comtessa . . . that Comtessa is the best of all of them. I never saw a woman so beautiful, or so beautifully dressed. You didn't see her eyes. She had eyes like carnelian. I've never seen such eyes. And when she kissed me—she smelled like perfume."

"She should have smelled like horse, if she'd covered as much ground as she was hinting," I said.

But my mistress just smiled bewitchingly, mockingly.

"You are too everyday, you old nanny goat. You're too coarse to understand. *She* is some kind of princess."

Then she told me to make sure I had something fine for her to wear the next day, though she couldn't make up her mind what. I sat up stitching at her palest lavender silk, which I always thought made her look like a sunrise, but she fretted and jeered at it come morning. Those people made her even more dissatisfied than had been her wont from the start. She suddenly despised pale colors—the company loved rich, dark hues, deep emeralds and topazes and rubies as an especial favorite—and she wouldn't be seen in gowns she had adored as little as a fortnight before; I dressed her hair three times before she would settle, and then she stormed around her tower room foaming with impatience, for the whole company slept late, and made no appearance at table or stable.

It was late afternoon before the Comtessa appeared, dressed like a hunter herself: in supple black leather and a black bodice embroidered all over with jet beads. My mistress, in the deepest pink she owned, looked like a bud rose trembling next to a wave of dark water. She showed her all over the castle—the pitiful ruins, the woods and weed-blown kitchen gardens, the fine chapel—and the Comtessa smiled at everything, a trifle superciliously, and refused to go inside the chapel. "When you have seen one backwater Khanduras chancel, you have seen them all," I remember her saying, remember, because I expected my mistress's choler to rise and for her to lose her temper with the creature. But my mistress tossed her head and said merely—

"It's a wretched place. I shall show you better." As though she hadn't gloated to me many a time before that it was one of the oldest in Khanduras!

All those early times she was with the Comtessa I shadowed them, as a maid ought to, saying nothing and holding my tongue—the Comtessa noticed me about as much as she would a tree rustling, which suited my purposes—and when I tried to put my lady's furs and cloaks on, I was violently rebuffed. My mistress did not want to ruin the line of her dress or hide the exquisite column of her neck or the ivory stretch of her bust, and I could hardly tell her that both would be goose pimpled into oblivion if she carried on much longer in the cold. To my disgust, the Comtessa was the one who took the fur from my hands and wrapped it around my mistress's shoulders: "Hide that beautiful throat," she murmured, "I am envious of the light that touches it," and my mistress blushed again and smirked to hide her embarrassment.

"As though there were any light in this miserable swamp," she cried out. It was the first time I heard her dissatisfied with the home she priced so dearly.

"I am envious of the shadows of Khanduras that nestle on your skin, then," said the Comtessa (ugh!), and her hand lingered in the sables around my mistress's shoulders. Later I said that I thought she would have plenty to envy in that case, as surely the swamp was one of the darkest places in the whole continent; and my mistress did not laugh or call me the prosaic nanny goat, but told me sharply to hold my tongue.

How merry those wretches made themselves in the Big House, and the Comtessa merriest of all, for she was a creature of many colors and changing moods: languishing and philosophical one moment, laughing like a maenad the next. Her courtiers worshipped her. My mistress, the baby among them in her youth and ignorance, copied their habits shamelessly. It hurt me to see her listening eagerly to the Comtessa arguing some learned point about the poets of Lut Gholein, or wars fought ages past in the Skovos Isles, when to her the poets of Lut Gholein and the wars of Skovos were all one: she knew nothing. I was the one who read all her books, as she declared that squinting over vellum would make her eyes cross-set. But if the Comtessa knew it, then aye, it was knowledge worth having; and "the Comtessa says," and "the Comtessa remarked" haunted all my days like a ghoul.

Mornings were the only time we had rest of them and their festivities. They slept late, which they claimed was the fashion, sometimes until nearly sundown: then they would hunt, and bring back deer and squab and hare from the forest. I knew them to play ugly, coarse games—for all they were supposedly of fine stock—tossing corpses at one another: feigning to bite on dead creatures and laughing, or taking the raw blood from the kill, which we all found disreputable and foreign and superstitious. How stupid and foolish we seem, reading back what I have written. Sometimes the Comtessa went with them, and then my mistress would go too, sitting sidesaddle like a lady, for that was how the Comtessa rode. Then their whole band would fill the run-down halls with feasting and dancing and singing. The Comtessa would announce my mistress the lady of the house and sit her on a chair bedecked in the Comtessa's own velvets. As the night wore on, my mistress would dance herself into exhaustion—would have danced all night if I let her—but I remained steadfast, the specter at the feast, I dare say. I am not being immodest when I say that I drew my share of ribald comments and flirting jests from the Comtessa's people, for no doubt they would have made them toward any young person who wasn't in that moment dandling her baby at her knee; for I was not a raving beauty at that time. My mistress was in a bloom so complete, so blissful, that to see her go from room to room was to see summer walking. When *I* looked in the mirror, I saw a careworn, bitter little hag—for woe and worry was a canker to my heart, and moreover, to any good looks I might ever have claimed; which did not make my lady more likely to take me seriously.

That was the first time I saw any hint of the fabled wealth of the Big House. My mistress lavished gifts on the Comtessa that looked like the ransom of emperors. When the Comtessa, laughing, finally thrust that grotesque ruby ring onto my lady's trembling finger, my mistress presented her in turn with a luminous green stone like foxfire that was half as big again as the ruby. Even the Comtessa could not help but admire this flawless treasure, but my lady called it a trifle, and meant it,

and gloated over that hideous ring in private. I sought relief in the fact that it was far too big for her little fingers to wear.

> WHEN *I* LOOKED IN THE MIRROR, I SAW A CAREWORN, BITTER LITTLE HAG—FOR WOE AND WORRY WAS A CANKER TO MY HEART.

My lady's family had gone from awe at these interlopers to fear and despite. The flow of their riches outward to these people had not helped. The servants likewise were caught betwixt loathing and terror, and so were the crofters. At first they thought nothing of it except that there might be a copper or two to spare for men who held the fine horses or ran errands, but they were superstitious in the extreme of such beauty and wealth, such dancing and wine, and it took only one murmur that they were a curse on the Big House for most of the crofters to shudder at the sight of their perfect faces. I say most, for some of the younger and more foolish in the village had their heads turned.

Knowing what I know now, I should have paid more mind to the stories that were being whispered—of girls and boys who hadn't been seen after some "last night," who were maybe in trouble, running and hiding from an angry sweetheart but still not turning up after days, or who had got drunk and fallen in a fen; but I had my own difficulties. The Comtessa was paying too many attentions to my mistress.

And how could she not? I admit her this, if grudgingly, that the Comtessa was more or less indifferent to the wealth my lady was hunting up from dusty corners and secret caches, but she could never have been indifferent to my lady's face. My mistress wore her most beautiful gowns, and more daringly so, every day; turned so incandescent at a compliment from the Comtessa that it hurt me to look at her; drove me to distraction not being content with the dressing of her hair, or of her jewels; seized by misery and tantrums by what now appeared to her a poor woman's portion of dresses and out-of-fashion cuts. It seemed to me as though the Comtessa was amused by her to start, but now had begun paying her attentions to which, had she been a man, the whole family might have objected. If only! But she was a foreigner and a wealthy noblewoman and might play as she pleased, and play she would—with locks of my mistress's hair, with the lace at the end of my mistress's sleeve, with the flowers my hands tucked in my mistress's belt. Finally, that high-bred interloper turned to myself, and when her eyes were upon me I knew I was lost. They were brown as a brook, those eyes, but with liquid red lights inside, like the oil blotted up from the rivers.

"How your chaperone looks at us," she began to say at my presence, or: "Your duenna does not approve of me."

"How ridiculous. She approves what *I* approve," my lady would say swiftly, "never mind her—she won't disturb us, and I need her by my side," which I loved, I *loved*, but the Comtessa would give a helpless shrug and smile her languid, lazy smile at me and say—

"No matter. The duenna is right. I might lose myself in your eyes, my darling friend, without that icy stare reminding me that I, the foolhardy Comtessa, dare too much!"

My mistress would laugh, but I knew that I was being told to keep my nose out of it. I was terribly scared of the Comtessa. For all her laughing, insinuating, elegant ways, she would look at my mistress with the calculating glance of a cat with a very plump mouse. How could my mistress not understand that the Comtessa often made fun of her ignorance, or figured my mistress as the butt of a joke? Except of course that she did it so charmingly, and stroked her thumb up and down my lady's lovely wrist as she did so.

Then came the day I had hoped and prayed for: the Comtessa said they had rested enough and would leave. They had tarried nearly a fortnight with us and wished to get through the mountain pass before the weather became too inclement to cross. My mistress would hear nothing of it. She declared the mountain pass already inhospitable and insisted that the Comtessa and her people should stay until the thaw. The Comtessa simply smiled, declared that she would hold a party to cheer my lady, and my foolish mistress thought she had carried the point.

I imagine now that this was the common way of the Comtessa and her scourge, to squat in one place for as long as they dared, then to leave before too many questions could be asked. I thanked the heavens above that they were leaving, but already misliked the stubborn cast to my mistress's face. She fairly cried with vexation over dressing for that party. She was just a girl, after all. I do not defend her, but I want to make it clear, before I outline what came later. Recall that she was the merest, silliest, most self-obsessed child under heaven: recall that these were her worst sins, before that night.

In the end, she wore white—the simplest shift of it in purest fine-weight cotton—virginal and girlish, except then she made me damp it, so that she might as well have been wearing nothing. I very nearly barricaded her in the room. She was excited to the point of frenzy: laughing at nothing, so beautiful and so wild of mind that it frightened me. I argued that she *hated* white; she said that nothing would bring her so much attention in that room of black velvets and silk. It was true, but I told her she was demeaning herself. I may have told her that she looked no better than she should be, but in sharper language, and she shocked me further by putting her arms around my neck and kissing me, and saying, "Let your mistress pass, nanny goat, and bleat at her no longer," in such sweet music that I do not remember anything except that I let her go.

The party was riotous—so riotous that I went to the other servants' quarters and told them to lock their doors and not answer them for anyone, especially if they were young and good-looking. The family had already retired with the priests. Nobody came for me. My lady retired to her chambers only an hour before dawn. I will never forget the sight of her. She was trembling; her dress was torn and her hair in disarray, and she was ashen—so gray-faced and childlike that I put her to bed immediately like a baby. When I undressed her gown from her, I found that it had been torn not on a stray nail but by what seemed like human hands—found one ripped edge spattered with what I thought was drying red wine.

"Poor daisy!" I told her, forgiving her everything in that moment. "Poor little daisy—who has battered you so?" And I mixed her a posset and made her drink it. She said so much that I hardly remember any of it, but I do remember that she said—

"Oh, Nan—oh, Nan, she said I should be a queen. She is right. I *wish* to be a queen. Nan, she showed me so many things," and wouldn't say what those things were, though gods help me I have an idea of them now.

In the morning, they were all gone to a man; and my mistress had gone with them.

I raised an alarm, and the whole of the keep was in an uproar. We were all in such distress that we hardly noticed that a few of the servants were gone too. The hall was festooned with leavings, rubbish, stale wine, refuse. Half of us were cleaning and the other half mad, trying to find out which way they had gone. Their horses barely seemed to have left prints. A thick fog rose over the swamps. The old trick of bride-theft seemed to have finally been played on the family in return for all its old crimes, and played on the most beautiful and infuriating girl in Khanduras, although the bride in this case had no doubt gone willingly. I tried to suggest otherwise, not even believing myself, and was roundly mocked for it. The priests prayed for my mistress's soul, and we all went out with lanterns, trying to find any trace of her.

I was raging in her tower when they brought her home—her only, with no sign ever found of the Comtessa or her people—barefooted, in her white dress, confused but unhurt, except for a shallow knife slit at the side of her throat.

She could not say if anyone had attacked her. I put her to bed and refused to let the priests bleed her more, and I thought that it was an ugly end to a dreadful chapter in our lives, hardly dreaming what repercussions it would have.

III.

My mistress was ill for weeks. The snows blocked off Khanduras. The swamp nearly froze. She was languid and weak. She wailed for me if I left the room, and clung to me at night. She stroked that ruby ring like a kitten. Often, she asked if the Comtessa had returned—with the trusting eyes of someone who expected that the time would not be *if*, but *when*—and was hysterical when I told her that the Comtessa was surely not to return our way, and if she did, would not have the doors of the Big House opened to her.

For many of the missing servants and the young crofters' folk had never come back. They found one bloated corpse of a young man when the snow started to thaw, with his neck broken open and an expression of horror on his face. I kept these tales from my mistress, who was growing paler and more listless by the day, who kept crying out "Comtessa, Comtessa," even when it was my arms holding her; a feeble shadow of the headstrong creature she had been before. I nursed her and called her my foxglove, my lily, my daisy, every sweet name, but she would burst out in wild sobs:

"A daisy—a lily—pah! When she called me her white rose, with ruby drops of blood upon it! I hate this stupid peasant place."

She was so ill that the sickness took the warmth from her hair and leached it from her skin. Her pale flaxen hair became the color of snow, and her skin like ice. The learned priests could not name her condition. Only her eyes kept their color, those velvety brown eyes I so admired.

I grew afraid that she would see the ruin of her beauty and go mad from it, but in the cold depths of spring she rose and stared at herself in the mirror. She had a thin, hungry look to her, and her skin now seemed almost translucent. All she said of her changed face was, simply, "I become myself," and admired her own reflection more than ever.

That was the hideous winter. Now I will write of the sins of the spring, and the hideous summer that burns upon us even now. I do not know how I will write, but I must. In the end someone will find out truly what she is, and my only hope for forgiveness is that I will assist that end, in some future I will never see.

It was a changed woman who got up from that bed. My lady said nothing of the Comtessa for weeks. I saw naught of that hideous ruby ring. I trembled in relief that she had forgotten that wretched ghoul and was now a sadder but wiser woman. I served her the choicest sweetmeats I could find—she toyed with all her old favorite foods now and could not be tempted by the most elegantly cooked chicken breast, or the most delicate soup—and I did anything I could to entertain her: read books I thought would interest her, passed on gossip from the village. Nothing satisfied her. I often felt the fury of her dissatisfaction. I could no longer argue with her, for I feared the damage a harsh word could do, and indeed I preferred her annoyance to her languishing.

One day she stood looking out her tower window at the chilly rain blanketing all her lands, and she said—

"She has forgotten me. She has forgotten her bloodied little rose."

I would have gladly strangled the Comtessa in that moment. But my mistress became thoughtful, not deranged. I wish now that she had become deranged. I wish I had not slavered after her patronizing smiles. She slipped away from me often—she had somehow grown able to step silently from room to room, with a tread no louder than a cat's—and I would find her suddenly in front of the mirror, smiling at her reflection; or sitting in a chair, staring at nothing; or worse, gone entirely.

Sleep fled from me. I began to sicken from a dread I could not name. The fault was mine. I was the first to tell anyone who asked that she was better, much better; and indeed she began to laugh again, but her laughter was much more dreadful than before. Her streak of indolent cruelty increased tenfold. Where once she would have slapped an erring maid, she now clawed the face of the poor wretch, leaving marks that never quite healed. Instead of boxing the ears of the hearth boy, I saw her calmly push him down the stairs.

I write in full honesty that I did chastise her, and meant to chastise her bitterly. Yet it was pitiful chastisement, and I could not continue when her gaze rested upon me. The old horror came rushing up. I was terrified for her. I was terrified *of* her. She took to taking hour-long baths—the slip of a girl they brought in to carry water from the well and boil it in the cauldron was kept busy every day, for my mistress complained of premature wrinkles, of age; I mixed up herbal remedies of every kind, but nothing suited.

Then came the day when I found her in the bath, together with the girl who carried the water. The girl was stripped to the waist, and her naked arm was extended in my mistress's grasp: the arm was slit from wrist to elbow and her blood flowed freely over my mistress's face, her neck, the very water of the bath. The girl must have been bleeding freely for whole minutes.

When my mistress saw my face, her own admitted no guilt, nor even shock. Her cheeks were scarlet and gleaming with blood.

"It's a secret remedy, Nan," she said. "It works, truly."

The girl was too dazed to cry out. I bandaged the slit arm, and I took her from the tower room with my mistress's mocking laughter echoing behind me. I took the girl back home to the village and told her mother that she did not suit and was not to come back. When I returned to my mistress, she was happy and radiant and pretty again, and she kissed me and called me "Sweet Nan."

I confess that even then, not only did I not

confront her with what she had done, but part of me rejoiced to see her looking so like her old self.

There is no excuse. I was half-fear and half-joy. The next time I found her in the bath with the cook's girl who scrubbed the buttery, the girl's wrists slit, my mistress masked in blood again, I bound this victim up the same as before and sent her packing to her mother with the same warning. I offered up my own arms—my lady slapped them away impatiently—and over and over, I found her with these dazed, wretched creatures, hypnotized I knew not how into standing like cattle with their vital blood pouring over my mistress's snow-white skin and hair. Not an hour later I would be there as she glowed with contentment and beauty, pinning back the sleeves on her gowns, smiling as though she were terribly pleased with herself.

How many girls who suffered this way to start with I cannot say. They are far away from their sufferings now, in any case. There had been fewer than ten by the time she killed the first one.

Yes, I knew she would kill one eventually, not from desire but from carelessness, and I don't believe her first murder was intentional. She had already bathed that morning—I had bandaged up her victim and put her to bed—so I did not expect her to bathe again, and this time my mistress did not bother with the water.

When I walked in on my lady at last, it was too late for her victim. Both the girl's arms were slit to ribbons, and she lay slack against the tub, draining into it like a slaughtered cow. My mistress was scooping up great handfuls of blood and patting her arms and her neck with it. As I stood there, all she said was, "Oh, Nan, do take out this rubbish once I'm done with it."

What did I do then? I removed her "rubbish." I wrapped the dead girl in sacking like she was laundry and deposited her in the cold cellar. That night, it was my strong arms who put her in the reeking midden and buried her deeply among all the old bones and kitchen trimmings. If you dug up the midden right now you would find her rotten corpse, though who would go to the midden so close to the tower I have no idea.

> **THE ARM WAS SLIT FROM WRIST TO ELBOW AND HER BLOOD FLOWED FREELY OVER MY MISTRESS'S FACE.**

Afterward, I lay in my mistress's bed and begged her, weeping, to never practice such evil again; I pleaded with her to tell me who had taught her such wicked tricks. In my misery, I railed against the Comtessa. My mistress petted me carelessly, then said, not having listened to me at all—

"'Comtessa.' Yes, that was her difficulty. 'Comtessa' of where, exactly? Noble blood—but a homeless wanderer, travel-stained. *My* blood is the heart's blood of Khanduras. She must have envied me my noble home and ancient seat." (How I doubted that!) "I have more rights than her to 'Comtessa' . . . no, 'Countess.' I am the flower of my lands, with its royalty in my veins. She knew *that* much. *This* for the Comtessa, says another Countess!"

And as I watched, she groped beneath her pillow and drew out that glowing carbuncle of a ruby ring: and she flung it across the room with such violence that the ruby actually cracked against the stone wall.

From then on, I was not to simply call her "my lady" or "mistress," but to humor her by calling her "Countess, the Rose of Khanduras."

Yes, I knew for months that she was mad. But it was something deeper than madness, more monstrous than simply lovesickness gone too far. I dare not name what the Comtessa was truly. I do not even think it matters. What mattered was that she, and she only, turned my mistress to a monster; a monster who meant to rule all that lay before her—greedy, foolish, ignorant child that my mistress still was.

IV.

She murdered again before spring turned into summer, and this time with intent. My mistress had formed a fatal obsession with bathing in blood, for which I had no doubt but that the Comtessa was the source, and a fixation that only pretty girls should serve her purposes.

I confess that she killed Alyce, the charcoal-burner's girl, and Millie, the dairyman's daughter. I know she killed the sister of the cooper, but I never knew her name, and I don't want to know now. She killed Mari, the shepherdess, and Sara, who came raging after Mari, and plenty more besides. It sickens me to write them down. Crofter girl after crofter girl, anyone with a fair enough face, came under her knife: girls who I recognized and had grown up with, or girls I had known in their girlhood, and many of them coming fearlessly . . . for I was the one who was trusted.

They should have known better.

The Countess killed them all and never knew any opposition until she killed the scullery maid, and that in some desperation, for the girl was a child and fairly plain-faced for all that. She slit the girl's neck and drained her into her bathtub, then sat lazing in the blood before being surprised by that fatal child, the hearth boy. The hearth boy, who I suspect had been lusting for vengeance for years, sprang at my mistress with the knife from his belt.

How do I know this? I was there; I struggled with the boy while my mistress plucked his knife from her ribs, and in all annoyance she snapped his neck with a blow. I saw the knife, and it went deep inside her, but the blood that came out was not like normal blood. It hung out of her chest like long, brightly colored ribands, trailing *with* her as she moved. I had not understood what she had become, and nor had I understood her inhuman strength. The blacksmith could not have shattered the boy's neck in that way, with his big fists like hams, and yet my mistress did it as though swatting a fly. Then she demanded petulantly that I slit the boy's neck too and empty him into the bath, so that he would not go wasted; but she was dissatisfied with the result, and afterward declared that while the blood of crofter girls

might be barely adequate, the blood of hearth boys disgusted her.

I hid both bodies in the cellar. They are there still, at the time I write this.

You may ask, *Why did you do it?* I answer, *Because she was my mistress, and I obeyed.* Perhaps I thought that if I proved my devotion to her, she would listen to me and stop at the last; that after an initial spurt of violence, we might work something out, something less grotesque, less dangerous, less so easily discovered. I, who had once pinned her by her wrists and called her a fool to her face! I was, and am, utterly degraded. Nor was I clever enough, who had been proud of my sense and cleverness once, for there were uneasy whispers in the keep about what was going on, and the servants refused to wait on my lady— my Countess—entirely.

The rest of the story is known around the village now, and I imagine will be told to scare children for years yet to come. But as I have started, I might as well finish.

The priests rose up in a body (they must have known everything . . . self-serving monsters that they were themselves) and told the family that she ought to be sent away; that she should be shut up in some convent or cloister, and have her life forcibly devoted to prayer, and another heir found in some other quarter. They did not accuse her of murder. That would have been beneath them. They were as haughty as my lady, after all. They dragged my mistress before them and, without making any honest accusation, told her that she would be packed off as soon as travel could be arranged and that letters had already been written to that effect.

My lady did not rant or rave. In fact, she seemed to take all this in good calm. I told her that she and I would run away, and she took that in good calm too.

Gods help me, I truly intended for us to leave. I thought it would spare the last of the village, so denuded of the girls I had grown up beside. I thought that if we took enough of jewels and rich gowns we might make it to a city and sell our goods and that she could remove herself from the sight of the peasants she so hated. That was how I thought I persuaded her. I thought that she agreed with me, but I should have understood the familiarity of the smile on her face: it was the same smile the Comtessa had worn when my lady begged her to stay out the winter in the Big House.

What the village now barely believes is all true. The next morning, the greater number of the priests were dead, and the family too—necks broken; throats open; their noble blood splashed uselessly over the floors and hangings. The servants and a few chaplains fled screaming from the Big House, and many of them are mad with terror still from what they saw, and cannot talk sense. I am sorry that there are any clergy left alive, but not sorry that they cannot do anything but gibber, for it serves my purposes. In any case, not a soul was left in the tower except myself and my Countess, examining her reflection in front of her mirror, squeezing clots of blood from her long white hair.

"There you are, Nan," she said, laughing. "I have been waiting an age. You need to wash my hair. How ugly and frightened my maid appears this morning! I would stop being so ugly immediately, if I were you. Understand that you are now the last beautiful girl left alive, my beloved."

And that was when I fled. I wish I could say it had been in pure terror, but part of it was how unbearable it was that she had finally called me *beloved*. I saw a future, like a witch or soothsayer, and rejected it.

My granfer has spoken in my defense. Even as I write, he has stopped the rest of the crofters from burning me at the stake. I lied and said I knew nothing of the murdered girls, and if I am believed or if I am not, it is no matter. The crofters all know what she has done and understand that she is no longer human. Many say they doubt she was ever human, but this is foolishness: she was the same as any other silly mortal girl before the Comtessa came to this benighted place.

The plan is that they will storm the keep at sunrise, with torches and pitchforks and oil. They have shovels and picks, and plan to dig a pit within the cellars of the tower itself, in the hope that the walls will encase her foulness within. They will not use violence on her. I have told them some details about the knife, and that I am not certain that their pitchforks will reach their mark, but they will bind her hand and foot and throw her into the pit, and cover her up with the Big House rock and Khanduras earth that she adores so much as her birthright.

I am tired now. I need strength for what is to come. I do not know whether my strength will falter or if the hideous love that even now threatens to master me will come to the fore. Perhaps the Comtessa will return, out of nowhere, and bear her off after all. You who read this will either know the answer to these questions already or wonder at the fate of the miserable monster who inhabited the tower— and the more miserable monster who served her purposes. The Rose of Khanduras, buried in the stones and mud. If they throw me in there with her, I will thank them for it. May the earth not give back what it has taken. I lay down my pen.

A Collar of Thorns

COURTNEY ALAMEDA

ILLUSTRATED BY
STANTON FENG

I.

In the depths of a cold winter's night, a child's wail cracked the silence.

Evelynne sat up in bed, glancing at the door, her heart throbbing fast. It was after midnight, and the castle lay as silent as the fresh snowfall. Nothing moved. Moonlight streamed into the room through tall windows, coating the furniture in silver light. Outside, the pointed teeth of the Fractured Peaks tore into the sky, glowing. Maleficent. *Sharp*.

Deep winter had come to the Peaks, and it was so cold that even Lord Cassander refused to sleep alone. He slumbered beside Evelynne, undisturbed. The servants had withdrawn to their chambers or huddled around the fires in the great hall with the hounds.

Another long, thin shriek tore through the halls. Evelynne pressed a palm against her breastbone, soothing her pounding heart. The cry sounded like a baby's, but that couldn't be right; there were no children in this castle. And at this time of night, no one would dare leave the warmth of their bed. Winter in the Fractured Peaks could reach indoors and steal the breath off your lips. It would kill a babe in minutes. Maybe less.

But perhaps the cries weren't there at all. Evelynne's mother used to call her *spirit-touched*: Evelynne saw things other people couldn't, heard things that weren't there. Sometimes, she had dreams of things that *had* happened or *would* happen . . . dreams that felt too real. Too true.

But when she was in Cassander's bed, all her dreams darkened unto nightmare. She hadn't slept well of late, not since she had been forced to marry him.

Evelynne shivered in places the cold couldn't reach. *It's just another nightmare*, she told herself, knowing she wasn't asleep.

Absently, she rubbed the itchy, dry spot between the first and second knuckle on her right hand, thinking. Wondering. No, *worrying*.

Evelynne hadn't wanted to marry Cassander. She wasn't Cassander's first wife; nor, perhaps, even his tenth. Nobody in the townships at the foot of the mountain could remember how many women Cassander had taken to wife. Nor, more gruesomely, could the castle's servants tell Evelynne what had happened to the other women. Whenever she asked, they simply looked at her with blank, confused expressions.

Yet ever since the wedding, Evelynne had dreamt of faceless women with thorny, writhing vines bursting from their bellies. Round abdomens split like overripe fruit, revealing strange, hard pits in the wombs. Her own eyes clouded like opals and small, button-topped mushrooms sprouted in the hollows of her throat and collarbones. She dreamt of briars growing from her bones, of breathing fungal spores like hearth smoke.

But worst of all, Evelynne dreamt of a pale-haired child standing in the snow, his eye sockets stuffed full of charred twigs. Tear streaks cut through the black ash that darkened his face. In those dreams, Cassander stood behind the boy, clutching the child's shoulder.

Something horrible was afoot in Cassander's castle—something the man refused to acknowledge or admit. If Evelynne wanted answers about her nightmares— answers about the man himself—she would need to seek them out on her own.

When a third cry reached her ears, Evelynne slipped from the bed. The cold breathed down the front of her nightgown. Gooseflesh rippled across her breastbone. With haste, she pulled on her dressing gown, wrapped herself in a heavy blanket, and stepped into a pair of fur-lined slippers. And even then, the cold found ways to drag its teeth across her skin.

She took a candle from Cassander's bedside table and lit it with the fireplace's embers. Then, steeling her resolve, she crept from the bedroom.

In the corridor, her lungs burned with each breath of icy air. Strange shadows danced along the walls. Dim light spilled through the windows in blue puddles on the floor. Cassander's sprawling castle had been cut straight from the side of the Fractured Peaks, and so these windows overlooked the valley below. On a clear day, Evelynne could see all the way to the swamplands, where Cassander's power crumbled.

Evelynne hesitated, clutching the blanket tighter. The infant's cries were clearer now, the sound forlorn, lost. Forgotten. Evelynne turned in their direction. Her heartstrings pulled taut. It was harder to be brave in the darkness, and the candle shed such weak light.

She started down a new passage, jumping at her reflection in a mirror. Here, statues emerged from the shadows, watching her with sightless gazes; suits of foreign armor glittered in the low light, their metal plates creaking in the cold. Grand tapestries hung along the walls, portraying battles she could not identify. Events she had not lived. Gods she could not name.

Evelynne hadn't been allowed to explore the castle—and while Cassander hadn't expressly forbidden it, his servants would always appear at her side when she wandered too deep into its corridors.

It's dangerous to wander alone, my lady.

The guards don't patrol this part of the castle, my lady.

No one is allowed in the southern wing, my lady.

It was always *my lady* and never *Lady Evelynne*, as if the servants had forgotten her name already. Or perhaps it didn't behoove them to learn her name at all if she would be dead in a year's time . . . or less.

Evelynne turned a corner, nearly screaming when she came face-to-face with a life-size portrait of Lord Cassander. She clapped a hand over her mouth, breathing deeply to steady her nerves.

There are no monsters in this place, Evelynne told herself, then repeated the words as she stepped past the portrait. The back of her neck prickled, as if someone had made a pincushion of her flesh. She glanced over one shoulder. The hallway behind her stood empty. At least, it *appeared* empty.

There are no monsters in this place . . . there are no monsters in this place . . .

Except for the one in her bed.

Evelynne followed the child's cries through the castle, memorizing her path so she might find her way back to bed: *down the hallway, turn right, walk past the portrait of Lord Cassander, left at the fountain.*

After what felt like an eternity of wandering, she walked into a forgotten wing of the castle, one with threadbare carpets, soot-darkened paintings, and tattered draperies. In this part of the castle, the infant's cries bounced from wall to wall. The shadows thickened, coalescing like dark clouds and stamping out the windows' light.

Every hair on Evelynne's body rose as she felt something watching her from the darkness. Dread pooled in her gut. The air grew stale and heavy, pressing on her from all angles, making it difficult to breathe. Her heart beat on her eardrums, *boom, boom, boom,* as a growl resounded from the darkness, sawing into her bones and her blood, splitting open her sanity like a seed pod and scattering every thought, every memory, every part of her soul to the void, as if it was ready to scoop out her heart and—

> EVERY HAIR ON EVELYNNE'S BODY ROSE AS SHE FELT SOMETHING WATCHING HER FROM THE DARKNESS.

"Evelynne!" someone snapped. "What are you doing here?"

She whirled, dropping the candle with a thud. Its flame winked out. The shadows rushed in like a wave, swallowing her whole. She gasped, holding her breath and waiting for a death that did not come.

Evelynne's eyes adjusted to the darkness, but slowly. She looked up. Lord Cassander stood ten paces before her, alone. The wan light from the windows outlined his square jaw and glimmered off the silver strands in his dark hair. It was impossible to guess the man's age—here, now, he looked to be in his early fifties. Handsome, but age had begun to take its toll. In broad daylight, he looked to be a man of no more than thirty. But in the firelight of his private study, Evelynne swore his hair looked white as the snowcapped peaks, and his brow just as craggy.

"I heard a baby crying," Evelynne replied, gesturing to the walls. "Did you hear it too?"

"On the contrary, the night has been unnaturally quiet," Cassander replied, crossing the space between them. He placed a firm hand on her lower back, guiding her from the hall. "The air is thinner here. It can cause you to see and hear things that aren't there—you know that much. Come with me. You will feel better once you're warm."

The child's wail rose again. "There!" Evelynne said, halting.

Cassander stopped and frowned at her.

"Can't you hear that?" she asked.

"No," Cassander said. "You are clearly suffering from some sort of delusion, Evelynne. Come! We must get you warm."

"But I—"

"*Evelynne,*" Cassander said in a tone that turned her marrow to ice.

She made no further protest, allowing Cassander to shepherd her away. Just as they turned the corner, she cast one final glance toward the empty hall.

A small figure stood in the window's failing light, no taller than a child. Though Evelynne couldn't be sure, it looked like a little boy with sand-colored hair. The creature cocked its head at her; then, before Evelynne could cry out, the boy hurtled backward, as if he had been snatched into the deep darkness.

Cassander said nothing, gripping her waist tighter.

Evelynne's cry died in her throat.

II.

Over the days that followed, Cassander refused to speak of the incident. No matter how Evelynne begged him to explain the baby's cries, the strange presence in his halls, or the women from her nightmares, the man would not relent.

You have nothing to fear, he would always say. It was a lie—of course it was a lie, crafted to keep her docile and quiet. But *docile* was never a quality Evelynne had possessed; she may have been raised to be a lady, but she wasn't a fool. She couldn't silence her sharp mind or deaden her instincts.

As the days turned into weeks, Evelynne took advantage of her every solitary moment to scour Cassander's castle for clues. She searched her chambers and Cassander's bedroom, running her hands over the strange trophies from foreign lands that littered the castle, hoping to hear an echo. A memory. *Something.* She looked through every book in Cassander's library; studied the tapestries; combed the guest rooms. But it was as if the castle had forgotten about the women who came before her, much like its staff had.

When Evelynne asked the chamberlain

about the infant's cries, he looked at her askance. If she questioned the lady's maids on how many of Cassander's wives they had served, they would blink and ask, slowly, *"What other wives, my lady?"* Evelynne thought she might be losing her mind.

At night, Evelynne lay beside Cassander in bed, worrying the little wound between her knuckles. No matter what the servants said, Evelynne *knew* other young women had been sent to Cassander. Five girls, perhaps ten in Evelynne's lifetime, all to be his brides. No one questioned Cassander; no one stopped him, because once the girls were gone, the memory of each one became as threadbare as a half-remembered dream.

Which meant no one would remember Evelynne either—not even her own family, nor the parents who had taken a bride-price in exchange for the life of their only daughter. Her parents had been kind people; perhaps they hadn't known they were sending Evelynne to die. Perhaps they thought they were simply doing their duty. Or perhaps Cassander had enchanted them too.

"Are you rubbing that sore again?" Cassander asked one night, looking at her over the top of his book. They sat in the solar as the last of the day's light slipped away. He, reading some esoteric tome in his chair before the fire; and she, pretending to work on a bit of embroidery on the settee. The servants moved about the room, pale and silent as ghosts, lighting candles and drawing the drapes over the windows.

"It's nothing," Evelynne replied. She lifted her embroidery frame from her lap, careful not to prick herself with the needle.

"Come here, let me look at it," he said with a sigh, setting his book on the end table beside his chair.

"It just itches occasionally."

"Come. Here." Cassander annunciated the words with so much ice, the servants in the room went still.

Unnerved, Evelynne dropped her embroidery frame back into her lap.

Cassander leaned forward, rested an elbow on one knee, and said, "Do not make me ask you a third time."

So she set her embroidery aside, rose from her seat, and went to him. She offered him her hand without a word. If she trembled, it wasn't from fear but fury.

Cassander took her hand and tilted it, examining the wound by candlelight. Small, pearly yellow blisters now beaded the skin between Evelynne's first and second knuckle. Several had popped, leaving gleaming, pinhead-size depressions in her flesh.

"Look at the way it festers!" Cassander's face darkened. "This may be symptomatic of something serious—I will summon the apothecary on the morrow. Perhaps she can give you a sleeping draught for your night terrors as well."

"Or you could tell me why I dream so darkly," Evelynne replied, slipping her hand from his. "I never had such dreams before coming here."

"The castle frightens you," he said dismissively.

"It doesn't," she replied, making fists with her hands. "I'm no fool—it's clear something is amiss in this place."

Cassander sighed, leaning back in his chair. "How many times must we have this conversation? There are no children in this household, Evelynne. No wailing infants, no young boys running through the halls . . . which is precisely the problem."

"And how many women have died to address this *problem*?" Evelynne snapped.

Cassander drew a sharp breath. With uncanny synchronization, all three servants turned their heads to look at Evelynne. For one brief, horrid moment, each seemed to wear Cassander's face. The temperature in the room dropped, and Evelynne's stomach twisted.

"Only the women in your nightmares," Cassander replied, rising. He towered over her, blocking out the light. Evelynne stepped out of his shadow, backing toward the door. "Had I but known you were touched like this, I would have taken one of your cousins instead."

Evelynne shuddered. "And when I die in the birthing bed, torn to ribbons by vines and thorns, will they be next?"

"Enough! You speak of something you know naught about," Cassander spat, then strode toward the door. "You are too quick to believe your own vain imaginings."

"Cassander—"

"I said enough!" He turned on his heel, glaring at her. And just before he left the room, he muttered, "No matter how many times I have tried to destroy the mistakes of my youth, they still bear fruit."

He left Evelynne in the solar, alone. As the cold crept in, so too did her doubts. *Had* other women been sent to Cassander, or was she misremembering? She racked her memory, struggling to recall the details about the others who had come before—the color of their hair, the shapes of their faces, even their names. But every memory she grasped turned to smoke.

Her confidence cracked like ice underfoot, threatening to send her tumbling into the freezing, suffocating depths below. Cassander was lying. He *had* to be lying.

That night, Evelynne kept herself awake as long as she could. She watched the moon rise through the windows and listened to the child cry in the distance. Evelynne believed Cassander when he told her there were no children in the castle; she *didn't* believe him when he said the infant's cries were delusions.

As she lay in bed, Evelynne rubbed the sore on her hand, trying to conjure a way out of the castle. She rubbed it until thorns sprouted from the skin and pricked her thumb . . .

Until the blankets on her bed turned to drapes of spongy moss . . .

Until the stone floor disappeared beneath the rising waters . . .

And until her bedroom walls crumbled away and left her in the realm of dreams.

Evelynne dreamt of a swamp. Or at least, she *supposed* it was a swamp. Having grown up on the flanks of the Fractured Peaks, Evelynne had never seen such a landscape before. When she stepped from the bed—now more of a mound of moss—she stood ankle-deep in a mire. Mud filled the gaps between her toes. Rotting trees rose from the murk, their trunks twisted, and great green banners of moss hung from their branches. Yellow fireflies danced over the water, winking at her like cats' eyes.

Evelynne found it difficult to breathe—the air smelled like a morning chamber pot and filled her lungs with a warm, wet stickiness. Fog reached its fingers across the water's surface, patchy and thin. Overhead, the stars glittered in the sky, their light cold and distant.

A short cry drew her attention left. There, a small figure stood in the shadows of an ancient, creaking tree. His pale hair glimmered in the fireflies' light, reminding her too keenly of the boy from her dreams—the one she thought she'd seen silhouetted in the castle window. He beckoned to Evelynne, then turned and disappeared into the fog.

"Wait," Evelynne whispered, reaching toward the child. Or, at least, what she *thought* was a child. With another glance around the swamp, Evelynne started after the boy.

Clad in only the woolen nightgown and the trousers she had worn to bed, Evelynne picked her way through the mire, mindful of her bare feet. Beyond the ancient tree, she found a solid, hard-packed path. It led her to a clearing surrounded by tall, shivering willows.

In the midst of the clearing stood a cottage built of stacked stones with a mossy, peaked roof. Light danced across the windowpanes. The chimney coughed out smoke. *Someone* was home, though the pale-haired boy was nowhere to be seen. As Evelynne approached the cottage, its front door swung open.

She halted on the path, uneasy.

A woman stepped outside, dressed in a mud-green habit fashioned from lumpy, hand-spun yarn. Oddments hung from her leather belt—including, to Evelynne's dismay, a thirsty-looking knife. The woman's graying hair was tied into a neat bun at the nape of her neck. She looked neither young nor old; and bright, intelligent eyes gleamed in her broad face.

The woman crossed her arms over her chest. "So, not all of Cassander's girls are useless, I see."

"Who are you?" Evelynne asked, glancing at the knife, then back to the woman's face. "I-I'm not even sure how I got here."

"Some seers can move through deep dreams," the woman replied. "By art or instinct, you managed to follow the warnings I sent you—the warnings I've sent all of Cassander's girls. Most were not clever enough to heed them."

Evelynne narrowed her eyes. "The nightmares came from *you*?"

"Indeed," the woman said. "But they are more than nightmares, because they are true."

"All of Cassander's wives have died those horrible deaths?" Evelynne asked.

The woman nodded.

"By his hand?"

"In a manner," the woman replied. "But you need not share their fate—I can give you the power to stop him, though it comes at a price."

"You didn't answer my question," Evelynne said. "Who are you? I have heard tales of witches in the swamplands, and none of those stories end happily."

The woman smiled, cocking her head to one side. "Aye, but a witch will speak the truth to you. Can your lord husband say the same?"

Heat flared in Evelynne's cheeks and breast. "Cassander is only my husband in name."

"Hmph," the witch replied, beckoning to

her. "Come inside, then, and let us talk."

For a moment Evelynne hesitated, glancing back the way she'd come. Nothing stood on the path behind her, nor stalked her from the shadows. Not even the little boy.

"Nothing will harm you in this realm of dreams," the witch said, turning toward the door. "Come."

I can give you the power to stop him . . .
Though it comes at a price.

At the very least, Evelynne would hear what the witch had to say.

The inside of the cottage was quaint: Bundles of herbs hung from the rafters, their varieties motley and wild. A local apothecary had taught Evelynne a few of them—mistletoe, vervain, and monkshood. They filled the room with the heady smell of licorice and summer wheat; of dusky, crumbling earth and lemony sunshine . . . and of rot, too. The large wooden table at the center of the room wore fresh bloodstains, though Evelynne saw no corpse. Nor bones or offal, for that matter.

A whole stack of books served as a makeshift table leg; scrolls were stuffed into the windowsills and piled on the floor. Writings rose in mountains by the fireplace. The mantel sagged under the weight of too many tomes.

Life sprouted in places the books were not: toadstools, delicate little purple flowers, and bulging, fat vines. Grayish-green in color and as thick as Evelynne's wrist, the vines had wrapped themselves around several of the rafters. She rubbed her knuckles absently, her sores pulsating. Her flesh had turned shiny and pink, like a fresh burn. A spidery network of crimson veins now stretched across the back of her hand.

The witch swept past Evelynne, heading for the fire.

"Why would you warn me?" Evelynne asked. "I thought witches never helped anyone, at least not for free."

"We aren't inclined to be charitable," the witch replied, using tongs to place another rough-hewn log on the fire. "But we may be able to work out a mutually beneficial arrangement, you and I."

"Such as?" Evelynne asked, though she wasn't entirely certain she wanted to know.

The witch clucked her tongue. "Years ago—perhaps *lifetimes* ago, who remembers these things?—your lord husband came to me, looking to strike a deal. He wanted an heir, but his wife was barren. You've heard tales like these before, haven't you? I gave Cassander what he asked for, but he refused to render payment in return."

Evelynne lifted a brow. "And what sort of payment was that?"

"A secret," the witch replied, lifting the lid of a pot that hung over the fire. She sniffed once, made a face, then set the lid back down. Straightening, she dusted her hands together. "One from his own lips. A bargain, really, considering the services I rendered."

"Did his wife bear a healthy child?" Evelynne asked.

"She did," the witch said with a sigh. "But there was no happily ever after for that child, nor his mother . . . nor for any of the other mothers who came after her . . ."

The witch's words struck Evelynne like a

bolt. She put a hand to her abdomen, glancing down. A tremor started in her heart, causing her muscles to quake. In her mind's eye, she could see the women lying in blood-soaked beds, their bodies torn open like the petals of gory blossoms.

In them, she saw *herself*, reflected a hundred times over.

"Cassander makes the townsfolk forget them, as you've no doubt noticed," the witch said, turning toward Evelynne. She lifted a finger. "But what if you could make his people remember their lost daughters and sisters, cousins and friends?"

"The people would think him a monster, if they could only remember," Evelynne replied. "They would tear him limb from limb. I would be free."

The witch smiled, but there was no mirth in her expression. No warmth.

"I'm not allowed to leave the castle," Evelynne said. "And even if I could, no one would believe me. I've searched the castle for proof that these women existed, and yet have come up empty-handed each time."

The witch considered Evelynne for a moment, then shouted, "Boy!"

A gentle rustling drew Evelynne's gaze toward the rafters. The pale-haired boy emerged from the shadows, staring at Evelynne with twig-filled eye sockets. He twitched, then cocked his head.

"The boy knows where Cassander keeps the townsfolk's memories," the witch said. "He's tried to reach them before, but Cassander thwarts him each time. With your help, however, we may actually succeed."

"How?" Evelynne said in a half whisper.

"Release the memories of the missing women," the witch replied. "Sow chaos in the castle, then break down the magical wards that protect Cassander. Bring him to me, *alive*, or close enough to it. Do this, and I will spare you from the curse growing in your womb."

Evelynne clenched her hand in front of her abdomen. For the past fortnight, she had felt the darkness spreading through her body, slow as the shadows creeping over the world at dusk. Cassander's poisonous seed had already taken root. Evelynne shuddered.

"There are leagues between the castle and the swamplands," Evelynne said. "How am I to traverse that place, pursued and pregnant, with Cassander in tow?"

"The boy has ways in and out of the castle, ones only accessible to someone with his unique . . . *condition*," the witch said, reaching up to pluck a few herbs from the rafters. "Do as I say. He will handle the rest."

In the rafters, the boy only grinned.

III.

As promised, the apothecary came the next morning with a poultice for Evelynne's hand. When Evelynne asked about a sleeping draught, the older woman looked at Evelynne sideways. "Whatever for?" the apothecary asked.

"Nightmares," Evelynne replied, trying to sound nonchalant.

Lifting a brow, the apothecary took a small, clear bottle from her leather satchel. "One or two drops will be enough to ensure a deep sleep," she said. "Any more than that, and you may not wake for a day or more."

"I'll be careful." Though Evelynne didn't intend to use the draught on herself at all.

After the apothecary left, Evelynne spent the rest of the day in the solar, reading a book by the windows. Or at least, her book lay open in her lap, but her attention was on the townships below. Dressed in snow and adorned with icicles, the city glittered. Smoke danced from chimneys. People bustled through the streets, greeting, hollering, and haggling in the market stalls. Well-dressed servants hurried to and fro. Children chased one another through the alleyways, laughing.

And Evelynne, trapped in the castle, could only sit and watch them. What would happen when they remembered their lost daughters? Would they rise up and tear down the castle walls? Would they demand Cassander's head for his crimes, or would they accept their fate and do nothing at all?

She lifted the draught bottle to the light, turning it to refract the weak winter sunlight. It would be difficult to slip even a few drops into Cassander's drink—the man was cautious to a fault. But if she could manage that, perhaps she could fulfill her half of the witch's bargain too. Assuming, of course, that memories of the dead stirred the townsfolk to action.

After dinner, Evelynne had the chamberlain bring a fresh-brewed pot of tea to the solar. The man set the tea tray on the room's sideboard table. Evelynne rose from her seat. As the chamberlain turned to draw the drapes over the windows, she slipped the draught bottle from her sleeve, uncorked it with her thumb, and put three drops of the clear liquid in one of the teacups. Enough, she hoped, to knock Cassander senseless for an evening.

As Cassander entered the room, Evelynne made a show of pouring herself tea.

He paused on the threshold, staring at her. The air prickled with static, making the little hairs on her arms stand on end. Her heart beat a little harder. She glanced at the chamberlain, who had gone still.

He can't know, Evelynne told herself. *Can he?*

"Tea?" she asked Cassander, trying not to sound too eager.

"Yes, please." Cassander glanced at the chamberlain, who hadn't moved. He frowned, then said, "The apothecary came today, did she not?"

"She did," Evelynne said, pouring a second cup of tea.

"And what did she prescribe?" Cassander asked as he settled into his chair by the fire.

"Exactly what you asked for," Evelynne replied. "A poultice and a sleeping draught."

"Hmm." Cassander lifted the teacup to his lips, inhaling its rising steam, then set it back on its saucer. He looked at her, eyes narrowing, as if he could flay her with a single glance. The fire in the hearth went cold. Time seemed to slow. And the chamberlain remained frozen by the window, one hand still twisted in the drapes.

"What did you put in *my* tea, Evelynne?" Cassander asked.

"Nothing," she replied. "I am well aware that you don't like sugar or cream—"

"That is not what I'm asking," Cassander said, his voice so low it could have scraped the marrow from her bones. He rose from his chair, hurling his teacup to the ground. Evelynne recoiled. "*What* did you put in my tea?"

Evelynne crawled off the settee, putting the chair between them. "I-I don't know what you're talking about—"

"Don't lie to me again," Cassander said in a half growl. He stalked across the room and grabbed Evelynne by her upper arm. When she tried to twist away from him, he dug his fingers into her flesh, drawing a pained cry from her lips.

"You put that sleeping draught in my tea, didn't you?" he asked, giving her a hard shake. Her head snapped back, sending a hot bolt of pain down her spine. He pulled her close, giving her no room to think, nor even to breathe. "Why?"

"I don't know what you're talking about—"

"This reeks of a Hawezar plot." Cassander dug his fingers into her flesh, the timbre of his voice hitting her eardrums like thunder. "What dealings have you had with the swampland witches? Tell me!"

With a shriek, Evelynne pushed him away and stumbled back, catching herself on the window behind her. The icy pane shuddered under her weight, but held.

"I've done nothing wrong," Evelynne snapped. "Unlike you, I have not sent countless women to their deaths!"

"If you are working with the Hawezar, you would send me to mine," he roared. "They are *enemies* of everything living, Evelynne! And without my protection, the people in these townships will *suffer*."

"You expect me to take pity on my *murderer*?" she spat, stepping toward him. Her breath sawed at her throat, painful and sharp. She swallowed down tears and said, "*You* have already condemned me with the babe in my womb!"

Cassander's eyes widened. He took a half step back, his jaw slack, as if Evelynne had reached out and physically slapped him. The color drained from his face.

> WITH A SHRIEK, EVELYNNE PUSHED HIM AWAY AND STUMBLED BACK, CATCHING HERSELF ON THE WINDOW BEHIND HER.

"You . . . you're pregnant?" Cassander asked her, his voice barely above a whisper.

She answered him with a glare.

"Whatever the witches have told you, it is a lie," Cassander said. "No matter what I do to protect my wives, the Hawezar always find ways to curse them. Each and every time. Who do you think is responsible for the infection now spreading across your skin?"

Evelynne glanced down at her bandaged hand. "And knowing that, you *still* take more women from the townships. You make the people forget us, so that they don't rise up and depose you—"

He narrowed his eyes and dropped his chin, glaring down at her. "Do you think the *Hawezar* will help you? They help no one but themselves!"

"At least *they* won't ask me to give my life for

a child I neither wanted nor asked for!"

Anger flashed through Cassander's eyes. He stepped forward, lifting a hand. Evelynne's chin quivered, but she forced herself to hold his gaze.

If he was going to strike her, he would do it while looking her in the eye.

"Do it," Evelynne said. "But if you would strike me, do it in the gut, where your blow might be of some use."

He blew out a breath, then dropped his hand to his side.

"You will not leave your rooms until the child is born," he said, taking her by the arm and dragging her into the hall. "If the child is healthy, and *if* you survive, I will decide what to do with you then."

Cassander locked her inside her chambers. When he was gone, Evelynne grabbed the vase that held her dried wedding bouquet and hurled it against the wall. Shards of porcelain and clumps of withered petals tumbled to the ground.

Evelynne collapsed to the floor and wept—not in sadness, but in frustration. In *fury*. At first, her sobs shook her whole body. As she quieted, Evelynne heard an unfamiliar rustling noise. The sores on the back of her hand pulsated and burned.

Wiping her eyes with the tips of her fingers, she glanced up. Movement drew her gaze to the pile of shattered porcelain and petals on the floor.

That pile *writhed*, rising and falling as if it had its own heartbeat.

Dread reached cold fingers through Evelynne's chest. Shivering, she crawled toward the wilted roses and brittle leaves. Plucking a large shard of porcelain from the pile, she cleared the debris away. The flowers disintegrated to the touch, dry and dusty.

And then, Evelynne saw the thorn.

It wasn't a snub-nosed rose thorn—this one was as long and thin as a needle. Trembling, Evelynne pushed more of the flowers aside, revealing a dry, leathery vine that twisted like a corkscrew. Evelynne had seen such vines before, wrapped around the rafters in the witch's cottage.

No matter what I do to protect my wives, Cassander's voice echoed in her head, *the Hawezar always find ways to curse them. Each and every time.*

The vine spasmed. Its putrid flesh oozed pus. Evelynne's skin rippled in response, as if something thorny and sharp wanted to push its way out, treating her body like the fertile grounds of the swamplands, feeding on her blood and sapping the strength from her bones.

With a shriek, Evelynne kicked the vine into her fireplace.

She took a shot of the sleeping draught and watched it burn.

Days passed in a haze. Evelynne curled up by her bedroom windows, too empty to cry. By day, she watched the townsfolk go about their business, each one ignorant of the horrors in the castle above. By night, Evelynne used her brooch pins to try to pick the lock on her bedroom door. Failing that, she took to searching the room's nooks and crannies, hoping to find a secret escape. She used candles to try to draw the attention of the townsfolk below; plotted to take one of the maids hostage; and even considered climbing out through the chimney.

In her most desperate moments, Evelynne dreamt her way back into the witch's swamp, only to find herself lost. Wandering. In the realm of dreams, the swamps teetered on the verge of twilight. Sometimes, Evelynne hid from the great, broken-backed stags, ones that walked on their hind legs. Other times, she sneaked past men whose bodies were threaded with thorny vines. Many-tiered mushrooms sprouted from their faces or torsos, and their skin had turned leathery and gray. They stumbled to and fro, blind.

Some nights, Evelynne saw the pale-haired boy in the swamps too. Whenever she tried to approach him, he would fade into the shadows, silent as a ghost.

But one night, almost a month after her confinement, Evelynne happened upon a group of mounted soldiers in the swamps. As she drew closer, she recognized the heavy fur coats slung over the horses' hindquarters, the men's tall black leather boots, and their standard-issue broadswords. *Cassander's men.* What were they doing so far from home? It couldn't be a regular patrol—it took weeks to reach the swamplands on horseback. Besides, Cassander's men had strict instructions to patrol the borders of his lands, but not beyond them.

If she dreamt true, it meant Cassander had dispatched men after he'd learned about the baby. The thought made Evelynne hate him no less; he cared only for a healthy child, not for her at all. Evelynne was merely a vessel, a means to an end, and nothing more.

So Evelynne did not shout a warning as the swamp rose to meet the men. Rotting hands and worming vines reached from the murk, ten, twenty, a hundred of them. They grasped the horses' legs and dragged the screaming creatures down, unseating their riders. Bones cracked, thunderous as a rumbling ice sheet. Torches hit the water and drowned. Men shrieked as they were swallowed up by the shadows, then dragged into the swamps' depths. A few bubbles popped against the water's surface, and all went still.

How many people would Cassander send to their deaths for this? How could one life, yet unborn, mean more than her own? How could it mean more than the lives of the men who had been swallowed by the swamp?

Evelynne found no answers in her dreams.

Months passed. She lost track of the days. Her stomach swelled. The infection spread up the back of her hand, pocking her flesh with sores, scabs, and blisters. Unless she could find a way to satisfy the witch, Evelynne was likely to become one of the shambling creatures from her dreams.

There was no escape. No hope . . . until one night, Evelynne dreamt of a door. She stood in a darkened castle hallway, alone. A small amount of light eked through the windows at her back. The dust hung thick in the air, coating her lips and tongue with a chalky residue. The carpet underfoot felt stiff with disuse, and Evelynne flinched as something large and many-legged crawled over her bare foot. She kicked it away.

Evelynne hadn't dreamt of the castle before. She looked left, then right, but the darkness hung like thick tapestries on either side. Cassander's servants could not follow her into her dreams.

Reaching out, Evelynne ran her fingers over the figures carved into the door's surface. On one side, angels bore shining swords, their wings streaming behind them. On the other, hulking demons roared their defiance, backed by flame. Two figures stood in their midst—an archangel and a demoness—locked in an embrace. The door told a story Evelynne hadn't heard before, one that must have been ancient.

From somewhere beyond, a baby wailed.

Frowning, Evelynne placed her hand on the door, covering the lovers with her palm. The muscles in her arm spasmed. She gasped in pain as something pricked her flesh from the *inside*, writhing like a worm. It broke through her skin, once, twice, then three times, shredding the bandages wrapped around her wrist. *Swamp vines*, growing from her hand.

The tendrils reached for the door, growing thicker by the breath, their tips burrowing into the crevices and breaking through the wood, searching, tearing, *cracking*, releasing something that had been entombed, and *oh!* Evelynne could hear the other women's voices now, rushing out from the cracks in the door in a rising chorus of pain and terror. Ten, twenty, then a *hundred* of them, all singing an aria of birth and death. The voices cried out for vengeance, swirling through her and past her, eternal and yet evanescent as they dissipated into the realm of her dreams.

The door crumbled before her, broken by the vines that grew from her arm. On the other side, there was naught but darkness.

"Evelynne, what have you *done*?" a man snarled.

Startled, Evelynne pivoted on her heel. Cassander stalked down the hall, his features twisted with fury and fear.

"What have you *done*?!" he shrieked. The windowpanes shattered, sending razor-sharp glass flying in all directions. Evelynne screamed as she dropped into a half crouch, protecting her head with her arms . . .

And then she woke with a sob, sitting up in her bed. The fire had burned low, throwing strange shadows over her walls. Sweat plastered her hair to her forehead. She struggled to catch her breath; her heart pounded in her ears, in the tips of her fingers, behind her eyes.

It was just a dream, she told herself, even as a tremor rolled through her muscles. She pulled her knees against her chest, and a single tear escaped down her cheek. *It was just a dream,* she told herself. *It was just a dream.*

One of the shadows in the room twitched.

She lifted her head.

> SHE STRUGGLED TO CATCH HER BREATH; HER HEART POUNDED IN HER EARS, IN THE TIPS OF HER FINGERS, BEHIND HER EYES.

The pale-haired boy stepped into the light, cocking his head at her.

"*C o m e.*" The boy inhaled as he spoke the word, stretching out the vowels in unnatural ways. His pitch rose and fell in the wrong places, the air playing his vocal cords like an out-of-tune instrument. He beckoned to her, then pointed to the bedroom door that hung ajar. A single key remained in the lock.

"Come where?" Evelynne whispered.

The boy took hold of one of the twigs in his eye socket and rolled it between his thumb and index finger. He tore it out with a fleshy, wet rip. He snapped the twig in half, dropping its pieces to the floor.

A heartbeat passed in silence.

Before Evelynne could ask anything more, shouts echoed in the distance. She kicked her blankets away and stepped out of bed, hurrying to the window. Below the castle, the townships blazed like a hellish inferno. No, *wait*—it wasn't the townships that burned. Hundreds of people marched through the streets, their torches bright. Men pounded the gates with a battering ram.

"They remember," Evelynne whispered, a gasp catching in her throat.

"*H u r r y,*" the boy croaked. "*N o . . . t i m e.*"

The townships' cavalry would come too late to save her, but perhaps Evelynne could still save herself.

With another glance at the door, Evelynne threw open her armoire. She found her warmest clothes by the weak light of the hearth: long woolen undergarments, a fur-lined shift, two pairs of thick woolen socks, and her heaviest petticoats under a quilted dress. It may have been spring, but the Fractured Peaks wouldn't know warmth until midsummer.

As she pulled on good, heavy boots, she heard Cassander shout, "Evelynne!"

"*C o m e!*" the boy said, beckoning to her again.

Evelynne snatched the bottle of sleeping draught off the table and followed the boy from the room. The hallway beyond lay empty. Dark.

"You little fool." Cassander's voice floated toward them. "Do you have *any* idea of what you've done?"

Evelynne's heart skipped a beat. She turned to face the sound of Cassander's voice.

He stepped into an island of light, a naked sword glinting in his hand. Evelynne froze. Perhaps it was the dim quality of the moonlight, but she almost didn't recognize him; he looked taller, somehow. *Broader.* Dressed in dark robes with his silver hair unbound, he looked like an avenging warrior . . . but the malice he exuded lodged itself in Evelynne's chest. No chivalrous force could feel so cruel.

Beside her, the pale-haired boy faded into the gloom. Evelynne eased back a step, draught bottle still in hand.

"First, I catch you plotting with witches," Cassander said, cocking his head, "and now I find you consorting with monsters."

"I suppose I've developed a taste for them," Evelynne replied, taking another step back. "After all, I had one in my bed not so long ago."

"Did you, now?" Cassander's lips curved like a reaper's sickle. "Then let me show you how monstrous I can be."

He leapt toward her, disappearing into the shadows of the hall. The vibration of his footsteps sent tremors through the stone floor. Evelynne shrieked. Grabbing hold of her skirts, she turned and fled. She sprinted down the hall, keeping one hand on her swollen belly, avoiding the windows' light. Her breath ached in her throat, and her legs—long unused to such activity—burned with each step.

Evelynne darted around a corner, not daring to look over her shoulder. Her mind ran as fast as her feet: She wouldn't be able to outrun Cassander for long, not while pregnant. How could she even hide? Cassander knew the castle better than she. Perhaps she could use the shadows to her advantage and take him by surprise. Topple a suit of armor in his path, or run him through with one of the swords on display in the great hall . . .

Pain exploded across the back of Evelynne's scalp. Cassander—*It must be Cassander*—grabbed her by the hair and yanked her off her feet. She shrieked. Bright red lights burst across her vision.

Before she could take another breath, Cassander grabbed her by the front of her dress, lifted her bodily, and slammed her against the wall. Her teeth rattled in her skull. Something cracked in her back and shot a white-hot pain through her rib cage, spearing the right side of her chest. This time, Evelynne didn't have the breath to scream.

"Contrary to your opinion, I don't enjoy watching my women die," Cassander growled, using his arm, shoulder, and hip to keep her pressed against the wall. Her toes did not touch the ground. "But *you*, well, you may be somewhat of an exception."

Evelynne struggled to breathe; everything in her chest felt like it had caught fire. With what little oxygen she could draw in, she cursed him.

Cassander threw back his head and laughed. The sound echoed down the castle's halls. Something within Evelynne broke—how she hated this man, the one who had turned her world upside down and made her life into a perfect nightmare, who would mock her as she fought for her life, who would laugh as she struggled to breathe. How *dare* he laugh! How dare he make light of the fear and pain he forced her to suffer.

With fury running hot in her veins, Evelynne smashed the draught bottle into the wall. Lifting her arm, she stabbed its broken shards into his throat, right above his collarbone.

Cassander's laughter died in a strangled wheeze. Hot blood splattered over Evelynne's hand. The man staggered. His sword clattered to the ground. Evelynne drove the glass ever deeper, soaking her bandages in his blood, feeding something cruel, dark, and horrible deep within her, something that burst from the flesh of her hand and wrapped itself around Cassander's throat, drawing tight. *Vines*.

"What . . . ," he gasped, but before he could finish the word, his legs went out from under him.

They tumbled to the floor. Evelynne landed atop the man, her right arm extended over her head. A fresh lance of pain shot through her chest. She tried to tug her hand away, but couldn't.

Cassander spasmed, then lay still. His heart still beat beneath her cheek, weakly.

Wincing, Evelynne propped herself on her elbow and looked up. In the hallway's dim light, she could barely make out the encircling vines that cuffed Cassander's throat, the ones that bound them together. With a sob, she tried a third time to tug her hand free. She only succeeded in driving the thorns deeper into her flesh.

Delirious with pain, Evelynne could hardly lift her head when the boy appeared from the shadows. Was it just her imagination, or did the boy grin? Did his teeth gleam, and had they been so sharp-looking before?

As Evelynne's consciousness began to fade, the boy took hold of Cassander's feet . . .

And dragged them both into the darkness.

IV.

Evelynne awoke lying flat on a hard, rough surface. She tried to open her eyes, but her lids felt leaden. Every muscle and sinew in her right arm ached. Pain hammered on the inside of her skull. She winced, turning her head to one side. Fire crackled somewhere on her right, filling the room with the choking scent of woodsmoke.

"Ah, you're awake," a familiar voice said. "You did well, my child, in bringing me both Cassander and his unborn babe."

Evelynne groaned. Cool air caressed the bare, swollen flesh of her belly. She shivered, but when she tried to reach down to cover her exposed skin, she realized her hands were bound.

"W-what . . . ?" was all Evelynne managed to croak. "What's . . . happening?"

"*Shh, shh,*" the witch said. "Take a deep breath now—"

A blade bit into Evelynne's abdomen, cutting deep. Pain exploded in her every extremity, erupting from her lips on a scream. Her eyes cracked open. The animal in her tried to tear free of her bindings, to twist away from the agony. But her hands and feet were held fast by vines—the same ones that twisted in the rafters overhead. She lay on the witch's wooden table. The witch stood over her, silhouetted in the firelight, carving a bright red gash into Evelynne's belly. Blood splashed in fast, hot rivulets down Evelynne's side.

Her vision swam, and her next breath was a ragged, beaten sob.

"Once more," the witch said, then cut the incision wider.

> THE WITCH STOOD OVER HER, SILHOUETTED IN THE FIRELIGHT, CARVING A BRIGHT RED GASH INTO EVELYNNE'S BELLY.

The pain shot up Evelynne's spine and hit the base of her skull like a battering ram. Evelynne screamed so loud, she thought her ribs might crack from the force of it; or perhaps the heavens would shatter and tumble down to the earth below. She arched her back, every muscle straining, the pain eating away at her sanity.

"P-please, stop," Evelynne sobbed. Tears gushed from the corners of her eyes, hot and fast as her blood. "*Please.*"

"*Shh,*" the witch said, reaching into Evelynne's flesh.

Evelynne felt something loosen in her abdomen. A small cry filled the cottage. The witch took an infant from Evelynne's body—a perfect child, a boy child, a *human* child—and cradled him against her breast. The child's cries carved into Evelynne's heart. She wanted to reach for him, but couldn't.

"That's not . . . what you said it would be," Evelynne managed to say. "A baby . . . Give me . . . my baby."

"You'll die before long," the witch replied.

"You . . . ," Evelynne said, nearly blind from the pain. "You did this to me, didn't you? The thorn in my bouquet. The nightmares."

"I *used* you, yes," the witch said, using the bloodied knife to slice through the umbilical cord. "But then again, so did he."

The witch stepped aside. There, sitting atop a stack of books, was Cassander's severed head. His blood stained their covers, turning black in the shadows. Perhaps she had gone mad with pain, but Evelynne swore Cassander's eyes blinked.

"He will make good on his promise now," the witch said, carrying the infant over to a makeshift cradle on the other side of the room. "Cassander was an Ancient, did you know that? Such secrets he will tell!"

Evelynne's world began to darken. "Just . . . before . . . give him to me."

"What's that, child?" the witch asked, looking over her shoulder. "You wish to live?"

Evelynne's lips parted, barely able to form the next word. Her breath was failing, her heartbeat growing ever frailer as her life's blood spilled across the floor.

"I can still save you," the witch said, her smile widening. "*For a price . . .*"

The Caravan

ADAM FOSHKO

ILLUSTRATED BY
ZOLTAN BOROS

I.

The weight of the sovereigns felt good in Jamir's satchel. It had been a solid season's work at sea, and he had been well paid. Tall and fit, the young man walked from the pier to the crest of the port overlooking the rest of the town. He could see the ancient citadel, the cathedral, and the rows of wealthy merchants' homes that lit the night sky with splendor. Below them, the markets, town square, and taverns were all alive with the sights and sounds of vibrant entertainment and the scents of exotic meats roasting in spices from distant lands. If only half of what Jamir had heard about Kingsport was true, this was the place for him to seek his fortune.

This was truly the crossroads of the world.

Jamir walked through the night with purpose. He caught the sweet and unmistakable fragrance of jasmine as several cloaked figures walked past him. A young woman with striking red hair turned as she walked, and he caught her blue eyes. She smiled. Someone—perhaps her younger sister—noticed this and started to giggle. But the moment was quickly broken by a stern look from what must have been their very pious and responsible governess. She regarded Jamir up and down with dour and deep disapproval.

"Come along, ladies! It is late!" the governess said tersely as she tugged at her own habit and hurried her two charges along into the night.

Jamir smiled to himself and kept walking. Night services at Kingsport Cathedral must have just let out.

He was going to like it here, he thought. There would be time enough for love, perhaps even a place in society, just as soon as he set himself up in this new place. The sound of Eleven Bells began to ring out in the town square, interrupting his musing. He was going to have to find lodgings and find them quickly.

Jamir changed direction and headed toward the taverns in the labyrinthine maze of looming buildings, houses, crates, and carts. The darkness of the night and density of the seaport fog wasn't making the navigating of the unfamiliar town any easier. But Jamir had spent most of his life at sea and in ports. There was little he felt he could not manage—even this pea soup of a night.

Walking by what looked to be a farrier's stable, several of the horses shifted on their hooves and marked their perturbance with grunts and snarfs. And there was another sound for a moment, too, one of shifting boots.

"Hello?" Jamir called out into the night. "If you would pick my pockets, show yourself!" A shadow seemed to pass quickly by, and some foul feeling came over him. He felt weak a moment, steadying himself against a feed trough. He caught the smell of wet grasses as he inhaled . . . and then something else. The smell of jasmine.

Then the dirty, cobbled street was gone. He suddenly saw himself a wealthy man. He looked into the eyes of his bride—it was the young woman whom he had seen earlier. Her eyes were the same. A moment later, he was older and had several fine sons. He was riding on horseback with his wife and their youngest: a daughter with her mother's eyes. And for the first time in a long while, Jamir was content.

He barely noticed when the knife slit his throat.

Jamir hit the ground hard. He might have seen the sovereigns raining down uselessly around him as the shadow fell on him, consuming him, swallowing him up, and literally starting to bleed the life's blood from his body. He might have, if his eyes had not remained fixed on this one moment of happiness in a far-off point in a distant future that was never to be. A sweet illusion.

Jamir only smiled as the light went out of his eyes.

II.

The next day, Rosie and her sister, Essie, played in the morning sunshine. They didn't usually venture far from home without their father, but today was different. He had been out all night hunting and clearing the traps of game. Mother allowed them to wait at the outer markers beyond the city gates so they could see him coming over the hills toward home, but Rosie had strict orders to watch after her younger sister. Unfortunately, Essie took every opportunity to live this hard-won moment of freedom to its fullest, starting with a colossal game of hide-and-seek—one that she was winning at the expense of her sister's nerves.

"Essie!" shouted Rosie. "Where are you?" Her cheeks were flushed with annoyance. She glanced around quickly—half looking for her sister and half expecting her furious mother to appear. "I don't want to play anymore!"

She waited.

Nothing.

Just birds chirping, which normally would be a sweet sound to her ears, but today Rosie felt like they were mocking her. "Did you hear me, Essie? I give up!"

Essie watched her sister from her hiding place, far off in the large tree at the very edge of the bend. Her fingers found the dark, charred edges where it had recently been struck by lightning. This was thought to be a bad omen, and certainly she would be disciplined harshly for getting so close to it, or even daring to venture out this far alone. But today, the risk was worth it to see her older sister in such a state.

Essie grinned from ear to ear and was about to call out to Rosie when she felt a shadow fall over her. She looked back and saw a giant staring at her. She screamed!

Hysterical, Essie fell out of her hiding place and plummeted to the ground, only to be caught by her ankle and then lowered gently. Despite this, she continued to gasp and whimper, terribly afraid.

"Stay back!" she cried. "Help! HELP! Rosie!"

A moment later, Rosie came running with the kind of protective fury only an older sibling can muster. But she fell stark silent at the sight of the huge man in the dark traveling cloak.

"I am sorry. It was not my intent to scare you, young ones," said the giant in a surprisingly pleasant voice. "I was afraid you might fall. Which, of course, you did."

"Only because of you! You . . . giant!" Essie shot back as she dusted herself off.

> ROSIE CAME RUNNING WITH THE KIND OF PROTECTIVE FURY ONLY AN OLDER SIBLING CAN MUSTER.

The giant smiled, relieved that the little girl had only bruised her ego. He seemed about to say something more when a deep, gravelly voice bellowed out behind him, "Romello!"

If the girls were disturbed by the large man, they were twice as disturbed by the appearance of his equally large twin brother. Dressed in an identical dark traveling cloak, this other giant didn't look down once at the girls. He only had his eye on his brother and the sun overhead.

"We have work to do, brother. The caravan is right behind us."

With a smile and a nod, Romello left. The girls watched the strange pair plod around the bend.

A moment later, the caravan appeared.

Horses, animals, and wagons covered in brightly colored fabrics passed by Essie and Rosie on their way to the large clearing outside the main city gates. Atop the wagons sat people of all shapes and sizes and walks of life. Some smiled at the two girls, some tossed them sweets, small flowers, and little gifts. And the music—the most joyful kind of strange and exciting melodies—seemed the perfect companion for a long train of traveling entertainers.

The trouble that had set these two girls off before was soon replaced by smiles and wonder. This was something they had never seen.

"When Father comes back, I want him to take us to see them," said Essie.

Rosie did not respond in kind. Something had caught the elder sister's attention.

"Listen . . . ," Rosie said, looking around. "I don't hear the birds anymore."

And it was true. They had stopped. And looking at the last wagon, they understood why. Set some distance back, the cart was covered in a strange, muted canvas and billowing silks. As it came closer, the wagon carried with it a chill that seeped deep into the bone, as if the very manifestation of death was gliding by. The driver, whoever it was—*whatever* it was—was masked and covered in black from head to toe. Even the horses tugging on the cart seemed gaunt and strangely melancholic as they trudged by.

Essie and Rosie suddenly felt something else, like the blackest curtain of night—silent, smothering, still—was falling all around them. As if the beating heart of life that they were so familiar with had been unnaturally suppressed.

As they stood shivering, they now became acutely aware of all the crawling things on the ground beneath their feet, every dry and desiccated leaf, and the vast cacophony of dead and dying things above and below—all reaching out, stretching, struggling, grasping—not for them . . . but for what was passing by.

III.

By the time night fell, the taverns were abuzz with news about the winding caravan that had set up just outside the city. Posters littered the town square, promising merriment and amusements from far-off lands. A number of the patrons had even caught a glimpse of two large twin brothers with a team of smaller men, setting the enormous pikes to raise the caravan's tents. Kingsport might have been an exciting place, but this traveling troupe was a mysterious and exotic addition with its own sights and sounds and smells, all of which seemed to intrigue the local inhabitants.

"They come from all over. Places I've never heard of," a voice said in the darkness. "Traders and performers, I hear. They even have a mystic who can raise the dead . . ."

"Are you listening, Seamus?"

Seamus opened his eyes.

He sat at a large open table at the far end of the Barking Dog. His clothes were not fine or flamboyant, but they were well made, belying his stature as the son of an enormously wealthy merchant. His handsome face had no lines on it, though there was an ever-so-slight hollowness to his cheeks.

His friends, the two flashy young men he was sitting with, had teased him about his plain clothes. But Seamus was hardly in the mood for fun. His mother had died some weeks back, requiring him to return to Kingsport from his studies. He was now caring for his reclusive tyrant of a father, who was as unpleasant and greedy as he was rich.

Seamus roused himself from his drink. "I'm sorry, what was that?"

"I said they can raise the dead," the young man repeated, reading off a parchment posting from the town square.

"Here now! Shh!" exclaimed a woman setting down ale mugs for the table, nodding to Seamus.

The first young man looked up. He had forgotten about Seamus's mother. "Oh. I—"

"It's all right," Seamus said, dismissing the hurt with a smile. He was used to it with these two, who often ate and drank like they had far more money than sense. Tonight, Seamus was just happy to be out. It seemed like an age since he'd been away from the oppressive mood around his family's villa. "Let me see it."

Seamus eyed the parchment. It was very theatrical, with archaic runes and symbols drawn around the edges. On the left side, images of happiness and light, sunshine and blooming flowers. On the right, images of decay and darkness, bones and mottled flesh. And in the center was a hand-drawn picture of a man—his face obscured but for his eyes, which seemed to burn through the paper.

And underneath it read: *Speaker of the Dead*.

Seamus smiled for a moment, bemused. "Well, this should set the local clergy alight."

Picking up his ale, Seamus sighed loudly, like a man wanting to forget his cares for a night. He raised the mug to his friends and the powers that be.

His eyes automatically wandered down again to the parchment. He read the large name written out on the paper. It said boldly . . .

IV.

"Zoranther!" called the woman. "Keeper of the Balance. Prophet and protector of the Cycle."

Ra'ael stood in the center of the tent. She was beautiful, riveting, powerful—in mind, body, and spirit. She let her words hang in the air for a moment. She could feel every eye in the crowd on her, as was her intent.

She imperceptibly noted the canvas folds flapping along the edges of their tent as more onlookers joined the audience. Ra'ael allowed herself to smile, ever so slightly. "Zoranther! Speaker of the Dead."

In that instant, the seven torches around the room suddenly burst forth in full fiery bloom with a flash and an audible *whoosh*. And there, standing in the tent, exactly where Ra'ael had been not a moment before—with not another soul around him—was Zoranther.

The crowd could barely register their shock before the man spoke. He was tall and lean, measured in his movement and speech.

"Tonight, I present to you our home . . ."

A curtain opened to one side of him, revealing a large, illuminated map of highlighted landmasses and seas, set upon a wheel with notches marked in the wood. "Sanctuary. Its ancient firmament possesses a wealth of secrets, many yet undreamt of. But at the center of this world lies its most guarded secret of all: the Balance between Life and Death."

> AT THE CENTER OF THIS WORLD LIES ITS MOST GUARDED SECRET OF ALL: THE BALANCE BETWEEN LIFE AND DEATH.

He stalked his audience as he spoke, measuring every beat.

"I have spent a lifetime searching for this knowledge," said Zoranther. "Paying a price few could comprehend." He locked eyes with a woman in the audience. "Tonight, I am ready to reveal its secrets and, in doing so, impart upon you its significance."

He reached over with his hand and pulled firmly on one side of the large map, sending it spinning like a wheel.

To the gasps of the crowd, Ra'ael appeared again and waved her bare arm over its surface, revealing intermittent flashes of silver where there had once only been empty notches. The reflected light from the wheel danced on their faces as Zoranther continued. "The Wheel of Life! And set deep within each spoke: the Seven Blades of Trag'Oul."

As Ra'ael stopped the wheel, she took a few steps forward, engaging the crowd.

"Each of the seven blades embodies the Cycle," she said in a deliberate tone, as Zoranther reached over and withdrew the first sword. "From Nothing to Life, when we are first breathed into existence."

"Amatosatratha," he said in a low, powerful voice, pointing the blade at a nearby urn. From the weapon, a warm energy washed over the room, and a sapling broke the surface of the earth, sprouting before the astonished audience's eyes.

Zoranther withdrew several more blades and called on their power as the sapling took shape, reaching toward the sky, splitting into branches, and bursting new shoots. "As we grow and bloom, we enter the Brace of Maturity..."

Ra'ael paused as Zoranther pulled another sword and pointed it at the plant. Again, he said a few words, barely above a whisper. This time the energy poured forth and enveloped the little tree. It grew and twisted and turned, becoming an enormous tree—its roots filling the tent and displacing more than a few onlookers. Their surprised clucks could be heard over the gasps of the crowd.

Seeing her moment, Ra'ael walked around the colossal tree that now filled the tent and took her place next to Zoranther, offering him another sword. "Then, like all things in this life, we wither. When our time comes, we pass under the Veil of Death." She handed Zoranther the sixth sword.

"Death is the natural end to Life," said Zoranther. "But those who know its secrets have an unnatural burden to bear. We must stand outside this cycle. Be responsible for it. But also become one with it."

He pointed the death sword at the plant, saying no words at all. From seemingly far away, a cold wind blew, and all that was warm and good was sucked from the tent. The twisting tree—once so full of life—convulsed, shrank, and died. This process continued until it was completely desiccated and dissolved into nothing before their eyes.

Mystified gasps filled the tent as Zoranther moved back to the great wheel. For a moment, just a moment, a young man caught his eye, watching him closely from the crowd.

There was something intense about this youth. A hunger.

But Zoranther quickly moved on.

V.

Seamus found himself strangely transfixed, compelled, by the scene unfolding before him. Right away he could tell that Zoranther was different than the others: all the conjurers,

illusionists, and soothsayers he'd seen in his Kingsport youth. He could barely recall their names or talents now. No, for all of this one's practiced stagecraft, there seemed to be a purpose in his patter. As if he was captivating the attention of his audience and keeping them riveted for some other, deeper purpose. And the girl . . . he couldn't tell yet what role she played, but Seamus couldn't wrest his eyes from them.

"However, lest you think this all mere theatrics," Zoranther continued, sliding the death sword home with a kind of finality, "Ra'ael, my apprentice, will further demonstrate."

The two of them shared a look. To anyone else it would barely be noticed, but Seamus could see in that glance an eternity of trust. Whatever they were about to do carried with it incredible risk.

"Are you ready, Ra'ael?" Zoranther asked.

"I am," she said as she again positioned herself in the center of the room. "Begin."

As Zoranther spun the Wheel of Life, the room darkened and thousands of tiny glints of silver filled the tent. Strange music floated above the crowd. Seamus could not see where it was coming from, but it was alluring and seemed to pass right through him. Looking up, he could see that Ra'ael was affected too, and she began to rise off the floor.

Bathed in a column of light, Ra'ael slowly turned in the air. Seeing her like this, Seamus now realized how young Ra'ael was. He was trying to place her age when the first convulsion hit her.

A ripple of alarm went through the crowd as Ra'ael was taken by the pain. "See how she dances with the wheel, as we all must. Leaving her youth behind."

Seamus looked again. It was true; the girl had aged twenty years in an instant.

The music intensified, and again Ra'ael was racked with another wave of pain. "But we are powerless to stop the Cycle, the advancement of age," continued Zoranther. This time she had aged another twenty years. Now the audience cried out. But Zoranther did not stop.

"The ravages of time are swift, and before we realize it, our time is nearly up." Ra'ael was moving far less; her hair had become gray and matted, her breathing labored. And still she turned. The next time the audience saw her face, it was that of an old crone, barely holding on to the thread of life. Each breath was an effort. And any moment could have been her last. Now the audience screamed for it to stop.

Not once.

Not twice.

But three full times, before Zoranther spoke again.

Even Seamus called out, digging his nails into his palms as he watched with furious intensity.

"But the power is hers. As is the wheel and the swords that drive it. Not because she tries to stop the flow, but because she is *one* with it," said Zoranther at last. "Because of this, she can come back from the moment of death and return to the strength of her youth."

A sigh of relief washed over the crowd as they looked again and saw Ra'ael slowly reversing in age. Her breathing had become calmer and more rhythmic, her face less a map of agony and ravage.

When her feet finally touched the carpeted floor of the tent and the last notes of the strange melody played out, the crowd could see that she was fully restored.

"For she has learned that it is not the power over Life and Death that is important, but rather the wisdom and knowledge to be the fulcrum that balances it. That is the way. That is the true power."

There was a beat—a long, somewhat uneasy silence that hung in the air—before the crowd spontaneously erupted. A rush of warm air filled the tent as it seemed to come alive, first with desperate applause and then excited cheers. Seamus rode the wave upward. He could feel the relief from the crowd, who had been held in such dire suspense. A few of the patrons had even passed out from the prolonged stress of it. This was catharsis. Even Seamus felt it, though he could not place *why* fully. He clapped loudly, and then whistled, as Zoranther and Ra'ael stood on either side of the slowing Wheel of Life and let the adulation wash over them.

It was the grand finale of grand finales.

VI.

After the show, Zoranther stood in the middle of the empty tent. He looked down at the trampled carpet. *So many lost people,* he thought. People searching. Not finding. Not even knowing what they were looking for.

He had been that way once, when he had another name. Another face. Zoranther turned and walked to the wheel, running his hand along the blades. Before he had been shown the truth and set on this journey. He wondered if his teachings had reached them.

"Where is the seventh?" a voice said behind him. When Zoranther turned, he saw the inquisitive youth from the crowd, now standing in the opening of the tent. "They are the *Seven* Blades of Trag'Oul," the young man continued. "There are even seven places on your wheel. Yet you showed the crowd only six blades."

Zoranther was impressed with his observation. "There *is* a seventh blade," he said, eyeing the youth closely. "But like the seventh state, it was not meant for man."

His tone was calm, pleasant even, but Zoranther had been around a long time. There was an intensity to this young man. He had spotted it very briefly earlier. And now here he was . . . These were not simply idle questions. This was need.

"Who decides this? What mankind can do or see? Or what will become of us?" asked the youth as he slowly walked forward. "Who decides our destiny? Is it not ourselves?"

Zoranther considered this as he watched the curious young man.

"What we do in the present certainly shapes our future," said Zoranther with a nod. "But, in my experience, there is far more to this life than what we see. Pieces in motion that we did not set. And some we cannot comprehend, let alone affect."

"I cannot believe that," he said flatly. The words seemed to burst out of him, catching Zoranther off guard.

Reading Zoranther's look, the young man seemed to calm a moment. "Please, excuse me..."

But Zoranther simply held up his hand. "No, continue."

The youth exhaled. "Sir. My name is Seamus. I have grown up in the shadow of my wealthy and successful father," he explained. "I feel it dogging my every step, the way he is trying to control my life. I thought it inescapable until tonight, but I know now that there is something else, a greater power..."

Zoranther watched the youth, trying to take him in as he spoke. Then he noticed his eyes going back toward the wheel and the blades.

"What I saw here has never been so... *real*," said Seamus, his tone growing more excited again. "The power of Life and Death."

There was a long pause before the young man looked back. "Will you teach me?"

It was a question that he had heard many times before. Zoranther studied the young man's face, searching it. And after a moment, he finally said in as compassionate a tone as he could muster, "I do not think so. I am sorry."

With that, he turned and walked back toward the wheel, removing the clasps that held the swords in place.

"What?!" sputtered Seamus. Zoranther recognized in it the cry of a desperate young man accustomed to getting his way.

"But—why not?" he said, walking right up to Zoranther as he worked. "I have the mind for it. I have studied. Scrolls and books and papers from the greatest philosophers. You cannot know!"

Zoranther stopped and looked at Seamus.

"I see in you the mark that consumes so much of mankind. A desire for life eternal, a lust for the power to command death."

"But you're wrong." The young man swallowed hard. "My family..." The words were hard for him to get out. "Has suffered... Someone... close to my heart." His legs were trembling now. Zoranther thought he might have to catch the young man, he appeared so shaken and weak. "If I could just—"

But for Zoranther there could only be one answer: "You have no balance. It is not in you. I cannot grow what is not there."

This hit Seamus hard. He stiffened. "If it is a matter of money..."

> "I SEE IN YOU THE MARK THAT CONSUMES SO MUCH OF MANKIND. A DESIRE FOR LIFE ETERNAL."

Zoranther would not dignify his words with an answer. Instead, he did something he had not done in a very long time. He looked at Seamus with pity.

That did it. Whatever facade Seamus was trying to keep hold of, it started to slip away. His cheeks flushed hot with anger as he took a step forward to try to grab Zoranther.

Zoranther stepped out of the youth's reach just when Ra'ael entered the room.

She quickly sized up the situation. "Is everything all right, Zoranther?"

Then, without even waiting for an answer, Ra'ael snapped her fingers. Almost immediately, the twin forms of Romello and Remullo appeared. The massive men dipped their heads as they entered the tent, but once inside they stood to their full, very intimidating height.

Seamus seemed to cool down; whether because of the implicit threat or just sheer embarrassment, Zoranther could not say. Either way, the youth nodded curtly to Zoranther and quickly made his exit.

The four of them watched Seamus bolt off into the night.

Ra'ael couldn't wipe the disgust from her face. "I hate the ones who hang around."

But Zoranther kept his eye on Seamus. "This one was different."

VII.

Seamus slowly made his way up the steps leading to his palatial family home. He was out of breath, only then realizing he'd run the whole way. He cursed having to flee from the caravan, but it wasn't the girl or the two giants who made him leave so abruptly. Maybe it was the shame. How had it all gone so wrong?

He took a moment and looked out over the estate. Even at night it was impressive.

In its day, with its many rooms, overlooks, grand halls, and vineyards, it had taken a hundred craftsmen years to build. And yet, in the blink of an eye it had seemingly collapsed with his mother's passing. Now the home was gone, but the house still remained.

Feeling more himself, he gripped the door handle and pushed his way inside, through the colossal doors.

Pools of candlelight did little to fight the vast darkness inside the cavernous halls. Seamus could make out the statues, oil paintings, and columns of rare imported marble—all plunder and spoils from his father's merchant and shipping empire. Right now, even the sight of it exhausted him. He just wanted to go to bed.

"Ah, the prodigal son has returned," a weak and sickly voice called from the darkness. "Look at you. Crawling . . . back here like a cat . . . in the rain—"

"That's enough, Father. I am going to bed." He turned and walked toward the living quarters. His face was getting hot again, and now his temples were throbbing. Seamus thought that losing his temper with Zoranther was one thing, but with his father . . . that would be something else. Better to withdraw.

"You are a fool, boy. Weak," he continued. "Just like your mother . . ."

This made Seamus stop dead in his tracks. The old man had gone too far. *What did you say?*

But his father just laughed. It was a bark of surprise, mixed with mock fear and mucous. More cough than true amusement.

For the second time that night, Seamus dug his nails into his palms. This time he stopped himself. Then he slowly said something he never thought he would say: "I am leaving."

This just brought more laughter from the sickly old man.

"Leaving? Oh no!" Seamus's father cried, his words oozing down the hall and into Seamus's ears. "You are my son. My legacy. My property. And you will never be rid of me."

VIII.

Romello stood on the far side of the encampment, closest to the city. He could see the lights through the trees of the forest. The evening was quiet. Dark. Calm. He liked it like this. Very often when the caravan would set up in a new place, he would be unsure of the surroundings or the people or the local customs. This caused him a lot of worry, more than he let on, but he had always been more sensitive to these things. Certainly, more so than his brother.

Here for some reason, though, he just felt at peace. Even his size didn't seem to be a barrier for once. Maybe, he wondered, if he and Remullo ever stopped traveling with the caravan, they could come back here. And then he would do what he wanted to do most—plant a farm, raise rabbits and maybe some livestock. That would be a better life.

A chuckle escaped him at the thought of this. It was against his usual nature, but he half wondered what his brother would think when he came back around the bend from town.

Even in the mist of the night, he could see the way. There was a burned tree along the edge of the path, its trunk twisted and its branches gnarled. He realized it was the same tree where he had seen the two little girls, just after the caravan had first arrived in town. As he considered this, a shadow seemed to pass over him, and he felt dizzy.

A smell then invaded Romello's senses. Earthy yet sweet, strong and unmistakable. Something he hadn't smelled in a very long time. "Chestnuts," he said, almost involuntarily. He grinned and walked forward, stumbling as he followed this intoxicating aroma.

As he rounded the trunk of the burned tree, the giant suddenly saw himself standing only a few paces away—by a blazing fire—and from it was coming the most wonderful smoke. He was humming a tune, something he thought he'd forgotten, and happily roasting chestnuts, which were popping and crackling in the heat.

Before his eyes, the scene changed and he saw himself again, not much older but more settled, walking into an enormous paddock of rabbits. *His* rabbits, in *his* paddock, on *his* farm, just as he'd always told his brother he would have. He loved these rabbits, and they loved him. He could feel it.

A moment later, the giant glanced down to see the two girls—Essie and Rosie, they'd called themselves—at his feet. They smiled up at him sweetly, neighbors come to visit his stock.

The first knife cut severed the tendon in his left leg. The second one, his right. The giant fell to his knees, still smiling—eyes fixed on a point in the distance. A vision of something that would never be.

He barely noticed when the knife slit his throat.

Romello never saw the shadow that labored over him, drinking his life's blood. And he never noticed his brother, half-buried under the leaves nearby.

IX.

Zoranther woke with a start.

He was still seated at his traveling desk, parchment stretched out, his quill loose in hand. He must have dozed off, he thought.

He'd had a dream of being alone in the darkness. Ahead of him was a large ball of churning fire on one side and a swirling ball of shimmering water on the other. And between them stood a figure, wearing a mask.

As Zoranther approached the figure, he found that he could only get so close—as if some unseen barrier cut between them. He called out to the person on the other side, but they did not respond.

Instead, the figure removed its mask. It was Ra'ael.

She stretched out her hands to either side of her, pointing to the large swirling orbs.

Almost immediately, the fireball leapt across the darkness and consumed her in a pillar of fire.

Zoranther tried to run forward but could not.

Then suddenly, the water sphere burst onto the fire, consuming it in an enormous churning waterspout.

When Zoranther looked again, Ra'ael was suddenly restored, as were the two spheres. She smiled and again pointed at them on either side.

He pondered his dream as he walked from his desk in the wagon to the dimly lit tents. But then something caught his eye on the ornate rugs that covered the floor. A slickness that blended into the crimson colors. He didn't need to touch it to know that it was blood—a lot of it—and that it stretched deeper into the room.

Zoranther followed it through the pools of light.

That's when he noticed that the cabinet by the wheel had been opened, the swords scattered on the ground.

He took a step but was stopped by a familiar voice. "Do not come any closer!"

Zoranther froze.

It was Seamus. "You know what I want. Now you are going to show me everything."

Zoranther peered into the darkness to try to locate the youth. "You know my answer. Why would I change it now, after this intrusion?"

An unspoken tension hung in the air.

"Because then I won't kill the girl," Seamus said, walking into the light. He held Ra'ael tightly with his own blade to her throat. His hands were covered in blood.

"You were right," Ra'ael said with icy calm. "This one *is* different."

Suddenly, the room was filled with laughter. It was terrible, sick, and self-satisfied. And it didn't belong to the young man with the bloodied hands.

As Seamus stepped forward, two gnarled hands opened the young man's robes from the inside. They revealed an old man's face and part of a torso protruding from his bare chest.

The skin between them was horribly stretched and marred, and the old man's mouth was damp with blood and saliva. The sight sickened even Zoranther.

"You should have listened to my son," sputtered the old man.

"Stop this. Please," said Seamus weakly.

"Oh, it will stop. Once this magician gives me what I want," cackled the fleshy face.

"I know what you have done," said Zoranther. "This is blood magic. Fringe sorcery. Twisted and perverse. It will carry a heavy cost."

His tone was even, though perhaps sad. Seamus's father was using him as a vessel, literally stealing the life from him. It must have taken great strength to resist his father's grip when the boy had visited him earlier. The inner fight between them must be terrible.

Zoranther had been right to regard Seamus with such pity; he just hadn't known why.

"Not *my* cost," the old man spat with worrisome glee. "The boy has been an adequate vessel for the necessary sacrifices to feed my condition."

The monster's yellow and bloodshot eyes suddenly shone with a kind of lust. "But now, with what you will show me, I will use these blades to restore myself completely. Then I can shake off this useless husk of a boy and have true revenge on my enemies! I will live forever."

The words fell at the feet of Zoranther. The old man saw this and got an idea.

"However, if I have not been persuasive," he sneered, "allow me to up the ante."

The blade being held at Ra'ael's throat moved suddenly and cut deeply. She said nothing. It was Seamus who screamed as her body fell to the floor.

Zoranther could hear Seamus weeping between breaths as the old man raged. "There! I give you this one chance! If you are truly what you say you are, you will take all you know, all your skill and learnings, and use the blades to restore her life! And I shall watch, taking from you your knowledge!"

Zoranther didn't move an inch toward his fallen apprentice. He didn't raise his hand to Seamus.

He simply stood there, took a moment, and closed his eyes.

This is what his dream was about: the choice he must make. He was the fulcrum. And balance had to be maintained. Whatever the cost.

He waited a long moment before he spoke.

"No," said Zoranther with finality. This was already a word the old man hated. Hearing it now made him seem to despise Zoranther even more.

"WHAT?! She is your student! You want to bring her back! You *need* to bring her back!" the monster seethed. "Do you not care what happens to her?"

"You don't understand," Zoranther said resolutely, though with a touch of sadness. "It is because I care that I cannot bring her back. I have walked Sanctuary for many centuries. I know what happens when the Balance is upset."

Zoranther looked down at Ra'ael. "But I *can* do this." He then looked up at Seamus. "Boy, do you wish to be free of this nightmare?"

"You will not answer!" the old man shouted as he tightened his grasp on his son's body, making him gasp in pain. Still Seamus managed to choke out a single "Yes . . ."

Zoranther closed his eyes and pronounced a string of ancient words under his breath. They had form more than sound, proceeding from Zoranther like a tectonic movement from the deepest parts of Sanctuary. Such were their power.

Whatever the response was, it was small at first.

Then it came in full.

The tent around them began to shift and flap, filling with light from a burning fire that was not there.

Seamus and the old man gasped as the Blades of Trag'Oul that littered the ground dissolved away in front of them, only to resolve again in their proper places around the Wheel of Life. A wheel that began to spin again on its own.

The large tent danced with a thousand shards of reflected firelight.

"What is happening?!" demanded the old man, his eyes darting in anger and what now looked like fear.

Zoranther turned to him. "What you have done is an affront to the Balance, the Cycle, and to my master, Trag'Oul . . ."

Suddenly, there was a sound behind them. Then one from the side. And then the other.

"You wanted life, and so you took it," Zoranther continued. "But those from whom you have taken, now demand it back."

With that, the half-decayed body of Jamir walked through the flap of the billowing tent. He was a true fright of ooze and worms. Though his face was now barely recognizable and his bones poked through his rotting flesh, the old man knew exactly who he was.

The monster recoiled and screamed, forcing Seamus to run to the exit on the other side of the tent. But as they were about to dart out, they were met by Romello. The gash in the giant's neck, though no longer pumping blood, opened and closed horribly as he shambled toward them, holding out his enormous arms as if to grab the old man.

Seamus stumbled backward—away from Romello—and right into the huge form of his very dead brother. He too had been slashed and bled. Though this time, Seamus could see right into his wide-open chest wound as the huge man grabbed him by his robes.

The monster made Seamus slash at Remullo with his blade, first at the dead man's hands and then his body. But it had no effect. Seamus stabbed more wildly, and the blade was finally lodged in the giant's rib cage. It then slipped from Seamus's grasp in the slickness and gore.

The old man roared his fear and frustration. Managing to get away again, Seamus and the monster inside him ran again to the back of the tent, but this time they were met by Ra'ael, her throat still oozing, her fingers sharp and fast.

She grabbed Seamus and the old man in an iron grip that held like justice. They struggled as the others closed in around them. Now there was no running.

Zoranther approached them with a look of final judgment. "You asked about the seventh blade. It is the Blade of Damnation. Of Living Death Eternal."

He produced the sword and held it before the monster whose greed had consumed so many.

"It was not meant for man. It was deemed too cruel," Zoranther continued. "But now, it

has found its match in you, vile one . . . and you have found your fate."

The words exploded in the ears of the old man. He looked deeper into the blade as Zoranther brought it closer to him.

Closer and closer.

Until he saw himself looking not into its surface but looking from the inside out. The old man screamed from his very core, and then there was a blinding flash.

When Seamus awoke on the floor, he felt as if an enormous weight had been lifted from him. With his father gone, he was now unshackled from the putrefying horror that had gripped his body and polluted his soul for so long.

Taking his first truly free breath, the young man looked up to see Zoranther, who smiled. "How do you feel?"

"Is it over?" asked Seamus, still bleary.

"Yes," said Zoranther. "That which was your father no longer corrupts you."

Seamus felt a twinge of sadness. To his surprise, a tear formed in his eye. The young man wiped it away. Or at least he would have, if he could move his arms.

"But the bloody hands that do the killing are as guilty as the heart, even in this matter," said Zoranther. "Balance must be restored."

It was then that Seamus realized that he was in a circle of some kind, drawn on the floor in blood. And everywhere his body touched its rings, he was held fast.

A rush of panic flooded Seamus. As his eyes whipped around the room, he saw the risen and decaying bodies from his earlier nightmares—the two giants, the sailor, and the strangely beautiful girl—all standing around him in mute testimony.

"And I must be the fulcrum." Zoranther sighed. "I am sorry, boy."

Seamus struggled. He tried to cry out. His mind flashed on every thought that sprang to his defense.

He barely noticed when the knife slit his throat.

Zoranther stood up, wiping the blood from his bone dagger. He looked into Ra'ael's cold eyes one last time. "This is where our road ends," he said. "Rest well."

She stood a moment longer, and then, as if satisfied, she and the others seemed to give up their animas—their spirits—and fall lifeless onto the floor. Zoranther regarded them as they lay on the blood-soaked carpet with a certain sad satisfaction. Their lives had been cut short so needlessly, and yet now they had also found peace—something that even he did not truly have. He felt a pang somewhere deep inside. Something indescribable. Yet he knew it was dangerous to envy the dead, and there was still so much to do. This would have to suffice for tonight.

He was done.

X.

Zoranther stood in the moment, surveying the crowd in the tent.

There was silence.

It was another town. Another night. But this night, his apprentice was not with him. He now did alone all the things that they had done together before. He spoke of the power over life and death, the discipline of what he knew as necromancy—and the importance of balance. This was the key, the vital thing that money could not buy, that the powerful could not control, and that force could not take.

But this was also the first night that Ra'ael did not push herself to the brink of death as she had so many times before, because she was now fully and deeply embraced by it. Instead, for the finale, Zoranther withdrew from the wheel the Seventh Blade of Damnation—intending to conjure forth the corrupted spirit held within it.

Zoranther was careful to point out that this spirit and its fate were both unusual. It was a rare thing for someone to be held outside of the Great Cycle of Life and Death. But so cruel and offensive to the natural order of things were this individual's crimes, that he truly deserved this equally cruel and unnatural fate. Zoranther never knew his name, just that a poor young man once called him father—and that this would be his final place of internment. Forever.

Zoranther then spoke the words . . .

What appeared before the crowd was more terrifying and bloodcurdling than anything he had ever shown before. The ghostly form of an old man's soul in searing, constant, and eternal torture issued forth, howling agonized screams and bitter lamentations. It was so horrifying, so gut-wrenching, so heart-stopping, that some people had to be carried out from the fright of it. That was one way to make them listen.

And so now there was silence. A gulf of furrowed brows, shocked stares, and held breath. But it was only for a moment.

For when the rush and roar of relief and amazement finally did come from the crowd, it was staggering. Even Zoranther was surprised.

> THE GHOSTLY FORM OF AN OLD MAN'S SOUL IN SEARING, CONSTANT, AND ETERNAL TORTURE ISSUED FORTH.

Zoranther thought about tomorrow, when he would load up his tents and move on to the next town. When this journey he had been set upon—his personal quest—would continue. And the caravan with all its secrets and stories would carve its way across the face of Sanctuary, like the very image of the great dragon Trag'Oul against the night skies.

In hope of saving more wayward souls and spreading the teachings of his kind, he would play the part of the entertainer for now.

Speaker of the Dead.

Prophet and protector of the Cycle.

Keeper of the Balance.

A Whiff of Salt

BARRY LYGA

ILLUSTRATED BY
JOSEPH LACROIX

I.

He came to me long past moonrise. Gallric, a relative newcomer to a village where newcomers are so rare as to be nonexistent. Five years he lived among us and still wore the label of neophyte. He kept to himself, worked a small patch of land, dug for turnips and beets, plucked wild mushrooms from the lower elevations. I knew him enough to nod at him in the market, nothing more.

And so I was astonished when I obeyed the midnight rap at my door to behold Gallric, his unshaven cheeks sallow and hollow, his gray eyes red-rimmed and fear-fissured. I expected to detect the reek of honeyed mead upon his breath when he spoke, but to my surprise, I smelled it not.

"I must come in," he said to me, his tone urgent and too familiar, presuming much on what was not even an acquaintanceship.

"Six hours to daylight," I told him. "I'll see you then."

"No. Now."

I stood athwart the door, uselessly, for he nimbly evaded my outstretched limbs and slipped into my hut, silent, ghostlike, treadless.

"I need a man of letters," he said, gazing around my abode, taking in my shelves of scrolls and tomes, meticulously and assiduously gathered over the decades. "I need someone who can write. Here, this means only you."

Sighing, I closed the door against the chill of night. "I was about to retire," I informed him. "On the morrow, I would be happy to write whatever letter or complaint you—"

"No letter," he said curtly, wheeling about to glare at me with those wild, crimson-webbed eyes. "And no complaint. We are all going to die; there is nothing for it. But something must be left behind. A testimony. A warning."

"All men die," I agreed. "But not now."

"Have you smelled it?" he asked, his smile both crooked and haunted. A mirthless thing, it was.

"Smelled what?" I replied.

"The air."

I allowed as how the air had taken on an unfamiliar savor recently. An almost pleasant tang that lingered in the cavities behind the nose just long enough to promise . . . something. And then, dissipation.

"Salt air," he said. "Smell o' the ocean."

The ocean. A hundred miles distant if a foot, to say nothing of the elevation. His comment wrested a chuckle from me, a laugh cut short by the brute seriousness of his gaze.

"I have never smelt the ocean," I told him. "I've never been. But I feel safe in saying that the ocean is too far—"

"The ocean is coming. Here. And thus, a testimony." He paced before the dying embers of my fireplace, restless and trembling like some creature both predator and prey. "A warning to others. Soon, we will all be gone. You must take it down. My story. My history. My pride and my pain. All of it."

I no longer hungered for sleep. I smelled again that strangeness in the air, as though the mere mentioning of it aloud had caused the scent to return. Could it truly be the ocean? Even here?

'Twas likely I would not recognize the scent of the sea, regardless. I have lived my entire life within a hand's span of the clouds, high atop the mountains that tower over the Dry Steppes, save for the youthful years I spent in the city, training in letters. And now, among the goatherds and shepherds and scrabbling farmers, my library is the field and the sky, the animals and their studied behaviors my laboratory. I am content here. I am known. I have nothing to fear.

Nothing.

And nothing would change that, least of all Gallric's dilated pupils and manic gesturing.

Still, to placate and assuage and perhaps out of my own curiosity, without another word I sat at my desk, gathering to me foolscap and my writing implements. I bade him join me at a chair nearby, but he shook away my offer with a physical vehemence similar to that of a rain-drenched wolf, standing instead where he could watch the fire and occasionally prod the logs into sparks and crackles with the poker.

And then, he spoke.

He spoke of the sea and of a listing temple and of something—of some *things*—that arose from the black and brackish waters. Once he began his story, the words flowed from him like the waters of which he spoke, without turning to me, without looking, without preamble and without surcease.

I dipped quill to ink, set ink to paper, to recount this tale as it was told to me. I have captured here faithfully what he told me, in his words, not mine. And I can promise only one thing: once read, whether you believe his tale or not, you will forget me and my small part in this, and remember only him.

And, I pray, his warning.

II.

I am Gallric. Gallric o' the Glade, Gallric Lightfinger, Gallric Swapcloth, Nimble Gallric. And more. And more they called me, in the city, in my time. When I was a younger man.

I never did learn how to read, how to make my letters. Never needed it. I learned all I needed to know with my hands, flash enough to pluck out any purse or wallet I could want. And my feet, fleet enough to run from the law. If there was something in the city someone wanted but couldn't have, they could have it from me, for the right clink of coin in my palm. And then there were the things I took just because I could. The city guards came to know my face. They knew my guilt, too, but couldn't prove it to the satisfaction of a magistrate.

I've said enough, maybe. Maybe I've said enough about all that. Except this: I robbed the local Horadric archive once. Got paid to take a bauble; took more'n one for my troubles. And that . . .

That . . .

I'd stolen from barons and earls, duchesses and even a princess once. But nothing brought the fires of the law on me like that job. You'd think I'd snitched Tyrael's wings right off his back.

So I scarpered. Too dangerous for the likes of me, and I had enough to live on for many and many a day. Packed up my loot, my coin, left everything else behind. Fled to Scosglen, out past the hinterlands, nuzzled against the ocean's breast. Druids founded Scosglen, they say. Nothing to do with cities and stones, streets and men's laws. Don't know rightly if I believe that or not, even now. Whether the Druids founded it or even if they existed. My whole life, I only ever believed in whatever I could pinch and stash in a pocket.

But . . . A safe place for the likes of me, I thought. A new place for my old face.

I stayed for a while, long enough to pick up the customs, the accents, the lay of the land. And then I went farther, out to the end of the world, where the land broke against the churning sea.

And then I went even farther.

> ### I ROBBED THE LOCAL HORADRIC ARCHIVE ONCE.

A little island just off the shore. Could barely see it with your naked eyes at sunup, if the mist weren't too fierce.

Even now I can't recall the name of the island and the name of the only town on it, a fishing village with more boats than men and a single alehouse to drown their misgivings.

The people there were simple folk. Simpler than me, at any rate. Which suited me just fine. They'd been on their piece of floating dirt for generations, and while they didn't take to newcomers all that well, they took to coin just fine. I spread some around and dug in in a little hut just outside the main fishing village. A copse of trees and a brackish stream between me and the rest of the world.

A strange coincidence of waterways kept the island in a thaw, when a place so far north should've been frozen over. Not that it was warm on the island—just warm enough.

So I'd done it. I'd lived the dream of every rogue and freeboot ever born: saved up my loot, kept my head down, and got out while the getting was good.

I was safe.

III.

Early on, I took to wandering a bit. I was restless in those early days, you see. Took years for me to learn to sleep at night and walk by day. Took just as long to stop looking over my shoulder. In my rambling around the island my first month there, I found an old temple a little deeper inland than most of the natives would dare go. To say it was in sad shape was to call the clouds white—it listed to one side, built atop swampy, broken land that could not bear its weight evenly. Its clapboard shingles had rotted from the salt air, built by someone who could not imagine the way the world corroded and corrupted even stalwart things.

> IN MY RAMBLING AROUND THE ISLAND MY FIRST MONTH THERE, I FOUND AN OLD TEMPLE.

Townsfolk said it was haunted. Said they were happy to let it molder and sink into the depths.

Like I said before: I never believed in nothing that could haunt. I had enough fear from those of the flesh and couldn't see borrowing any from the departed. But I needed a place to hide my stash, and it wouldn't do to hide it in my little hovel on the edge of town. My new neighbors were afraid to go near the old temple. One night, under a gibbous moon that could barely pierce the gloaming, I picked my careful way through the marshes and the reeds and the trees. The temple stood there, slick with swamp-sweat and the piss of a thousand herons and egrets.

The inside was just as rotted and fetid as the outside. I pried up some floorboards near the crumbling altar and hid my stash there. It was mostly coin and jewels—I'd cashed in or pawned most of the artwork and such before fleeing. But there was still one thing I'd held on to, from the Horadric archive job, the little extra piece I'd taken for myself in those dusty old archives. No one wanted to exchange coin for it, and truthfully, I'm not sure I would have parted with it for any sum.

And I don't know why.

There was nothing special about it. It was the length of my forearm and the span of a goblet at its widest. A stone statuette of a woman, arms raised. She was naked, but I'd seen enough women in the altogether that this wasn't what drew me to it.

There was just something about it. It had a dull patina to it, its surface pitted by water and wear. The closer I looked at it, the more details I saw: Sharp teeth, like a wolf or a shark. Long, winding tresses that at first seemed matted and dirty, but with a good, close peer turned out to be intricately rendered strands of seaweed.

It was ugly and it was beautiful all at once. Maybe like my own soul. I came to realize that it was my good luck charm. I'd never reckoned by such things before, but I'd taken it from the archive and gotten away scot-free. Made it all the way to safety. No guard on my tail; no one following me.

It was a token of my last job, and it kept me safe.

I left it with my stash in the temple at first, but I kept thinking about it. Almost like it called to me. So one moonless night, I went back to the temple and brought it to my hut. I slept better then.

But the people in the village had odd notions about privacy and thought little of entering someone's home unannounced. You'd think a thief would appreciate this quality, but I found it disconcerting. And besides, I was retired and I didn't want questions if anyone came to my abode. So I returned the idol to the temple.

And then... I missed it again. It was *mine*, and I deserved it, no? Went back again—another moonless night—and set it up in the hut again.

Went through this cycle many times. Bringing it to me, at peace, then slowly, over time, becoming more and more paranoid that someone would see it, that someone would try to steal what I'd honestly and rightfully taken. So I returned it to the temple in a safe spot next to my stash, until the next time I needed it again.

This went on and on. I came to accept it. It wasn't the worst way to be safe.

IV.

One day, as was my wont, I stood at the edge of the beach. A great pleasure of mine back then was standing at the waterline, where ocean kissed earth, and staring out at those great foaming, churning waves. I was a city boy, mind. Until coming to this island, the largest body of water I'd seen was a bowl of soup.

Cold salt water ebbed and flowed, eating at the chilled, dark sand between my toes. Not far from me, a man launched his fishing line into the water over and over, catching nothing. I watched him idly, one eye on him, one eye to the horizon. Somewhere out there—a day or so by the oar—was the mainland Scosglen, and somewhere deeper in, the Dry Steppes and even the city. There was so much land and sea between us that—

A sound off to my left pulled me back to the present. The fisherman had cried out in surprise. His line was taut and vibrating like a bowstring on the nock. The rod bent almost double, and his heels dug into the wet, giving sand.

I ran to him without a thought. In my younger days, I'd've run the other way, but I'd since learned to lend a hand. Kept people from being suspicious.

"It's fighting me!" he cried, feet slipping toward the brine.

I threw my arms about his waist and dug in on the more solid ground behind him. Through his body, I felt the struggle—the sea, the fish, the tide.

He leaned into me, bracing against my body. I thought the rod would snap in half, but he tilted forward, then back, keeping the fish in play. I inched away from the tide, and he followed, and with a long, steady, dedicated rhythm of back-and-forth and back some more, at last the fish exploded up from the salty water, as long as my leg and then some.

The sudden eruption caught me off guard—I let go of my companion and fell backward. He fell forward, landing close to the fish itself, which had beached and now flopped in the sand.

I collapsed, unable to find purchase to rise. Everything around me was too soft, grainy and unstable. By the time I'd regained my footing, I saw the fisherman on his knees before the fish.

I didn't know much about fish, even having lived on the island for a few years. But I knew this much:

They were only supposed to have *one* mouth.

And that mouth wasn't supposed to speak.

Yet, as I closed in on him, I saw even clearer the first mouth situated in its usual place, gaped and gasping, seeking water; and the other, along its flank, filled with dozens of needle-slender teeth and uttering words.

"... blasphemy ... engulf ..."

I stared, aghast, but more possessed of my mind than the fisherman, who could only gawp at the thing.

"Listen," the fisherman whispered, his jaw slack, eyes unblinking.

I didn't want to listen. The sound of its voice was like bee stings in my ears.

As I said, I knew little about fish, but I knew an abomination when I saw one, and I knew, too, how to deal with abominations.

I stomped on the damned thing, right in its center. My heel came down hard in the middle of another word—"*cru*"—and the thing's viscera exploded out of its face and tail. There was a pulped mash of dead fish beneath my heel, its guts twisting in the sand.

The fisherman stared, open mouthed, at me. No words passed between us. With our feet, we nudged and kicked the dead thing back into the water.

V.

That night, I drank at the alehouse. Most of the local men did, and a few women too. There was little else to do in the village, especially if you had no family. In the city, I'd never tippled—too afraid to lose my edge, my vigilance. But in my years on the island, I'd learned to enjoy the ale old Thorvaln brewed behind the alehouse from fermented kelp.

My idol was at the temple, and I was starting to think I might need to see her soon.

It, I mean. It, of course.

In a dark corner sat the fisherman I'd been with earlier in the day. From the look of him, he'd been swimming in drink for hours, but I noted only the one tankard. According to Thorvaln, this was the only one he'd served.

I went to the fisherman's table, back there in the dark.

"Ten words . . ." He was mumbling. "Ten words of terror it spoke . . ."

He muttered under his breath eight words he had heard just himself, then the ones I'd heard too: *Blasphemy. Engulf.* They lacked power, spoken in a voice other than the fish's, but clearly their hold on him was strong.

Then I noticed his tankard was still full. He'd had not a drop to drink, but his eyes bore the haunted and glassy sheen of a man in his cups.

Suddenly, he threw the tankard at the wall and screamed: "*Ten words! Ten words of terror!*

They're coming! They're COMING!"

Babbling nonsense now, his words inchoate and incompetent, he rose. Tears streamed down his face, and he began coughing, as though something had stuck in his craw. The patrons edged to the walls as the fisherman, now clawing at his throat, stumbled his way to the door and outside.

I followed. Mist had rolled in, gray and needle-cold. The fisherman collapsed to his knees a few paces from the alehouse door, hands still at his throat, as though to choke himself. I approached, wary. The mad are a harm mostly to themselves, but in their throes can hurt those surrounding. And I had made a life out of avoiding hurt.

He keened, long and high-pitched. I stepped closer.

And then, as I watched, he dug his fingernails into the soft flesh of his throat.

I froze there. Bubbles of blood welled up at the ten points of his fingertips. A steamy hiss escaped his lips.

I was helpless to stop him as he tore his throat wide open. I could only watch as his breath and his blood and his life erupted from him, and I could swear there was a satisfied smile upon his lips as he died.

VI.

Couldn't sleep that night. I'd lived my life on the free side of the law but had avoided violence wherever I could. Bloodshed was not my forte. I only carried a dirk for jimmying open windows and jewelry boxes. I could hardly throw a punch.

I couldn't stop thinking of his throat, of its yawning, endless gape. The ravaged vocal cords and the spill of blood . . .

The morning brought a new surprise, this one less bloody, but more mysterious.

Down at the shoreline, not far from where a pathetic streamlet joined the ocean, a misshapen dune had arisen overnight. It stood not quite as tall as a man and had the shape of a dome. Something too perfect about it rankled. It was made of sand but seemed a blight on the beach, unnatural. I didn't want to step near it.

Nor did anyone else, though for different reasons.

"It's a message from the Druids," someone breathed.

A murmur of agreement shuffled through the crowd. The Druids. The founders of Scosglen, if you believe the old stories. And my neighbors surely did. Founded Scosglen and—local pride insists—spent a moment just to the north to raise this very island up out of the waters and the murk.

Likely story. I'd more believe some demon had shit the place out.

No one would go near the sacred dune for fear of displeasing the Druids. Me? Me, I stayed away because I'd learned long ago to keep my distance from mysteries and things that I didn't understand. Best way to stay alive.

Everyone meandered away, back to the village, a prideful babble on their tongues. I stayed a moment longer, staring at the dune.

VII.

Days later, again at the shore, I beheld a new and unbelievable sight. If not for the fact that others witnessed it too, I would have assumed it to have been a dream, that I'd fantasized it. Or that my mind, tired of decades of switchback thinking, had given up and begun that slow maunder toward the dementia of the aged.

But others were there. They saw it too. We saw it, and we heard it.

The terns twisted above, their tails tilted as they flew. When they cruised low and close to the water . . . when they flew low to snatch up a fish . . . you'll call me mad when I say it, but I saw it *with my own eyes* . . .

> IF NOT FOR THE FACT THAT OTHERS WITNESSED IT TOO, I WOULD HAVE ASSUMED IT TO HAVE BEEN A DREAM.

As the terns closed on the surface, fish *leapt from the water*. Opened their mouths. Clamped hard on wing and leg and beak, and bore the terns down into the wet.

I *saw* it myself. I saw the fish, leaping with bloodlust, dragging their prey into the water.

A flurry of feathers flew, fell. The skin of the sea went white with them.

And then red.

Blood-soaked feathers drifted in on the tide. A harsh wind blew.

"The Druids are angry!" someone cried, to a chorus of tearful agreement.

I wondered if that could be. But I also wondered: What if this wasn't because someone was angry?

What if this made someone *glad*?

VIII.

I awoke that night to perfect stillness. As though the silence had somehow stirred me from a perfect slumber. I waited, listening.

And then when I needed to inhale again, I realized what had awakened me.

A *smell*.

The sea.

The ocean's pleasant salt tinge had gone brackish and too pungent. From aroma to stench.

I lit a candle, hoping the smell of tallow would drown out the permeating scent of something bitter and rotting.

But a candle could not ward off the unease that crept along my spine like a column of fire ants. I'd survived the city by obeying my gut, and now my gut cried out for escape.

Was it time to go? I thought of my stash hidden in the old temple, of the substantial amount of coin still available to me. Of the idol I had not held or beheld in so long. I had built a quiet, boring life for myself in this village, one I was loath to surrender.

I held no superstitions, unlike the fools in town who spoke increasingly of the Druids and their return. But as the people seemed to turn more and more toward the old ways, I knew it might become . . . uncomfortable for me. Inhospitable. The beach near the sand pile had become a moat of offerings to the Druids, beseeching their favor and compassion. People noticed I hadn't made any offerings. No one had said anything.

Yet.

I resolved to think more on it in the morning.

I waited too long. For the next day, the Examiners came.

IX.

I do not know who summoned them. It doesn't matter, I suppose. Someone spooked by the strange goings-on at the water, perhaps, who'd sent word to the mainland.

First, I beheld them at a distance, two tall and strong figures, so unlike the islanders who were all stooped by age and lifetimes at the rod and the net. They entered the alehouse.

I did not.

Strangers. On the island. It could mean only one thing: I'd been found out. Somehow, the city guard had stalked me here. It took them years, but they'd found me.

My fears seemed justified moments later. I found a young boy near the alehouse and summoned him to me.

"Boy, tell me—who are these strangers among us?"

"Other than you, you mean?" he asked.

"No sass, young crab," I told him. "Who are they?"

He shrugged. "They said they're Examiners. From the Horadric archive."

And with those words—*the Horadric archive*—he drove a spear through my heart.

They'd found me.

I thanked the boy and returned to my hut. I would have to go. There could be no doubt about it. When night fell, I would repair to the temple, gather my things . . . I could steal a boat—a small one, to be sure, all I could handle—and row to the mainland by morning's light.

A knock at my door interrupted my planning. My heart thrummed. The villagers rarely knocked. When they did, it was as they opened the door and cried out the "Ahoy ya!" greeting-warning.

But my door did not open.

Another knock.

I considered doing nothing.

"Gallric?" It was an unfamiliar voice with a familiar accent—the inflections of a city dweller, the cultured tones of an educated man.

I said nothing.

"We were told the man called Gallric resides here. May we enter?"

I had but one window, and there were two Examiners. Obviously, one was watching the window.

To my surprise, they both stood at the door when I opened it. I could have gone for the window after all.

To my further surprise, one of them was a woman, the heavy gray coat and men's trousers she wore obscuring this fact from afar. Her hair—the color of ginger—was tied back tightly, bare, unlike her companion, who wore a pointed cap. (Always respected women who wore trousers—more practical than dresses and skirts.)

"Who are you, and how do you know my name?" I demanded. Better to attack than to be attacked.

"I am Xoff," said the man, bowing slightly

and somewhat reluctantly, "an Examiner of the Horadric archive. My companion is—"

"I am Da'an," the woman interrupted, not bothering to bow. "Similarly associated with the archive. We were tutored in their ways abroad. We are from far beyond Istani."

"You've answered half my question," I said curtly.

"Thorvaln in the alehouse gave us your name," said Xoff. "May we come in? It's cold out here."

It was. The air had gone damp and chilly. Misty. I wondered if they could taste the tang of the bitter sea air like I could.

I allowed them in, then positioned myself by the door to facilitate a hasty exit if needed.

"I am told," Da'an said, after glancing around my hovel, "that you were with Stavrik—"

"Who?"

Xoff chimed in. "The fisherman. The one who reeled in the—"

"Oh. Yes. I didn't know his name."

"Really? It's such a small island . . ."

"I keep to myself."

They exchanged a glance.

"You were with him," Da'an continued after a moment, "when he caught the fish. The one with two mouths."

I had been interrogated any number of times. Long experience had taught me that it's best to pretend to be helpful. Tell every truth you can afford. It makes the lies go down easier.

"Yes."

"And it spoke. Stavrik told many others that it spoke."

"Ten words of terror," Xoff chimed in.

"Did you hear these ten words?" Da'an asked.

"This is why you're here?" I could scarcely believe my luck. They were not here for me at all. "Because of . . . a fish?"

"A fish that *spoke*," Da'an snapped angrily.

"Don't forget the two mouths," Xoff said, smirking.

"And you've no . . . strange desires, after hearing this fish speak?" Da'an asked.

> TELL EVERY TRUTH YOU CAN AFFORD. IT MAKES THE LIES GO DOWN EASIER.

"No urge to rip your own throat out?"

I coughed at that moment. Not for any reason related to their questions, but rather because the stench of the sea had caught in my windpipe.

"The air is getting worse," I muttered, clearing my throat.

"I myself smell nothing," Xoff commented. "I have daubed under my nose a tincture of my own concoction, a solution of oil of peppermint and—"

"The fish," Da'an interrupted. "Did it do anything else other than speak?"

"Only die," I told her, and then explained how I had crushed it with my foot and kicked its carcass into the sea.

"Do you still have that shoe?" she asked.

I blinked at her in confusion. "It's on my foot," I told her.

With a cry of triumph, she dropped to her knees and bade me lift my shoe, only to rise again, disappointed, at the discovery that the past days of sand and water had washed away any lingering guts.

"You'll have to forgive Da'an," Xoff said, now leaning against the wall, arms crossed over his chest. "My companion believes there may be . . . supernatural goings-on here in the village, and she is eager to find proof."

"The *fish*!" Da'an exploded. It was obviously a disagreement they'd been having for some time. "How can you doubt—"

"A mere freak of nature," Xoff said smoothly. "No mouth—a misshaped set of side gills widened by catching on the fisherman's hook. The 'words' it spoke being nothing more than gasps, misheard by our friend here and the one now deceased."

I did not think that to be the case, though now that he said it, I devoutly hoped it to be true. I had no stomach for magic or mysticism.

"The smell!" Da'an demanded, gesturing toward me. "He mentioned it. And everyone we've encountered says it's gotten worse!"

"No doubt some large fish—perhaps even a whale—has died nearby. I suspect its corpse will bob into view any day now."

"The sand pile!" Da'an went on. "The fish catching birds!"

With that, my stomach sank. There could be no rational explanation, only the supernatural.

"Equally explainable," Xoff said easily. "The sand pile is, I admit, too regular to have been crafted by the tides, but I surmise it was formed and placed by human hands—a local youth, pranking the spooked and frightened adults. As to the fish attacking the birds . . . A fluke of nature. We know that there are fish that prey on other fish; we know, too, that some fish can survive a limited time on land. Is it so impossible to imagine a predator taking advantage of the proximity of new prey?"

Da'an stared at him for a long and silent moment. "You are insufferable," she said. "And your hat is ridiculous."

"What does my hat have to do with any of this?" Xoff shouted.

He would have said more, but Da'an cut him off with a curt and sharp glare.

"One final question," she said to me, as Xoff folded his arms over his chest and fumed. "Have you heard bells, of late?"

"Bells?"

Xoff snorted. "Bells."

"They use bells," Da'an insisted.

"Say the old witches' tales and superstitions," he retorted.

They? I wondered. My curiosity perked up. What could *they* mean? Who were *they*? "No bells," I said. "There aren't even any on the island that I know of. The big fishing boats use drums to signal the shore."

Da'an stroked her jaw. "The barman. Thorvaln. He told us there is an old temple with a belfry. Out in the swamps."

My blood chilled at the mention of the temple. My stash! I knew the bell ropes had rotted through even before I'd gotten there. But—

"And I suppose you want to investigate

it," Xoff said. They spoke as though I'd left the room.

"I'm sure someone can—"

"I can guide you there!" I told her, hoping not to look *too* eager.

I couldn't let them go with someone else. It would be too risky. By going with them, I could guide them away from my stash.

Soon, the three of us were deep in the fetid murk of the inland swamps. It reminded me of the sewers back in the city, dark and wet and rank places I fled to when needs drove. Once upon a time, I imagine there would have been a clean path from the town to the temple, but it had overgrown and vanished long before I'd arrived here. Still, I knew the way, following a briny twist that broke the land.

It took us the better part of an hour to reach the temple, but at last I clawed a drapery of hanging mosses out of the way and there it stood. The mist had thickened, needle-sharp and pungent; heavy condensation blackened the boards of the temple.

"Túr Dúlric architecture," Da'an said breathlessly. "Dates back to the early Druidic period. There will be a bell in the tower. It's said that they use bells to—"

"For the love of Tyrael, old tales and myths are hardly enough to—"

Da'an seethed. "Myths can have teeth. They can bite."

Could they? Like every other gutter whelp in the city, I'd been raised on tales of the mysterious and magical, but I'd never paid them much mind. Ethereal goings-on were for others. I lived in a world of grime and crime. I didn't know who to believe—Da'an was forceful and bright, but wouldn't a mage (as Xoff clearly was, to my eye) know the difference between true magic and happenstance?

Da'an had walked ahead, fuming. I approached her and asked: "'They?' Who are *they*?"

She said nothing for a moment as we picked our way through the undergrowth toward the temple. Then: "Have you heard of the Drowned, Gallric?"

"The Drowned?"

"Creatures from the deep. Servants of some ancient creature whose name we no longer know." She paused, thinking. Not to recollect—I knew she had all the facts on her lips. She was wondering how *much* to tell me.

"Once they lived as we do," she went on in a halting tone. "Men and women and children alike, innocent and guilty and in-between. But then something reached out from the cold black seas and took them, turned them into something foul, undead, undying. A submariner army of deathless loyalty. Every so often we hear of them, coming to the land to replenish their numbers, bringing the stench of rot and the strangest of phenomena with them."

I stared, dumbstruck. There seemed to be nothing to say.

And then from behind us, Xoff laughed, a short, sharp blurt of mirth. "My partner believes old witches' tales, I'm afraid. She sees ghosts and ghouls round every corner."

"Only around the darkest corners," Da'an

shot back. And then, to my surprise, she began to chant:

> Speaking in waves, oh, the Drowned!
> The Drowned will come upon the sea.
> Kelp-kilted, brine-blooded, moon-mad and wet,
> Upon the sea the Drowned will come.
> Oh, the Drowned, speaking in waves!

"They are not to be trifled with," she said, her tone so dark and serious that even Xoff could not find it in him to laugh. He merely gazed about the ruins and the marsh.

We had gained the door. I led them inside and discovered a six-inch-deep pool of water across the entirety of the floor. We sloshed as we entered.

Xoff made a gesture with his hands, and suddenly there was a pale ball of light floating above eye level. Da'an did not react, and Xoff obviously wanted me to, but I refused to satisfy him.

The inside of the temple was as wrecked as the outside. The floorboards did not so much creak as bend at our tread. The altar had begun to sag from its waterlogged foundation.

Water rose above my ankles. I kicked at it, a slick blackish spatter rising into the light from Xoff's magic.

"This wasn't here before," I said, more to myself than to them. I hunkered down and scooped up some water, dipping my tongue into it. *Ugh*.

"This is salt water, not marsh water or rain," I told them.

"So?" Xoff spoke; Da'an was staring around the inside of the temple.

"So, how did it get here from the ocean?" I asked.

Xoff chortled. "How long have you lived here, Gallric? Don't you know about the tides?"

I knew a little of the tides, of course. Enough not to be dragged out to sea by them. But not much else.

He continued. "Given how low this island sits in the sea, a strong enough tide could reverse that sad little creek we followed here. Push seawater along that channel, right back here."

I remembered, then, some talk in the town recently. The moon and the sun in alignment, highest high tide in a century . . . Something like that.

I was a trained scofflaw, and so I managed not to react when Da'an sloshed her way across the floor and trod directly over the spot where I'd hidden my stash. Xoff stayed at the doorway with me, not willing to wet his boots further, it seemed.

"The stairs to the bell tower are that way." I pointed. "They were still in reasonable shape last time I was here."

"Reasonable!" Xoff barked.

"Come along, you coward," Da'an grumbled, and led him away.

I waited until the creak of stairs told me they were nearing the second story. It was torture, but it also gave my old thief's eyes time to adjust to the magic-less dark.

Then I quickly splashed through the water to the spot where I'd concealed my treasure. The salt water had warped the boards somewhat, so it was difficult to pry up the flooring, but I managed.

Above me, I heard tread on creaking boards still untouched by the flood. Xoff and Da'an.

Soon enough they would realize the bells here were useless and would descend.

Working quickly, I set aside the boards. More water gushed up from beneath. My leather sack of coins and gems lay nestled where I'd left it, its stout cords tied tightly shut.

But there was no idol.

I pawed at the water, stirring it, feeling around, my fingers pleading to brush against its stone curves. But nothing. It was gone.

XI.

I no longer cared who was right—Da'an or Xoff. No longer cared whether it would be better or worse to have this isle assailed by magic or by simple logic. No, I lay awake that night pondering not the mysteries of the sea but rather *what had happened to my idol*. Who could have taken it? And what sort of person would take the idol and leave behind a sack of coin and jewels worth more than the entire island?

I'd managed to replace the flooring before Xoff and Da'an returned, bickering and insulting each other, angry over the fruitless trek through the swamps and perilous climb up the rotting temple stairs, only to find a rusted-out bell that could not have sung a single note even had its ropes been intact.

They debated again the whole way back to the village. My head spun between their arguments. Had I really heard the fish speak? Was I going to become another superstitious islander, making offerings to Druids I didn't really believe in, just in case?

More importantly, what had happened to my idol? I itched with knowledge and ignorance—it was gone, and I didn't know how or where to find it.

Maybe something magical *was* afoot.

I thrashed against my thin sheet, twisting and turning in bed like a newborn. Nothing made sense. The world was topsy-turvy, and the only comfort I found was in the lulling background noise of the surf in the distance, the steady tidal *thrum-crash, thrum-crash*.

And then I knew. I sat upright in bed, shocked by the obviousness of it all. There was no magic, no Drowned, nothing supernatural at all. I knew where the idol had gone.

So I went to retrieve it.

It was damn near impossible to see. The fog had gotten worse since the sun had set, and there was no moon. Chips of light fell from the stars. I had no torch because I didn't want to be seen.

My eyes soon picked up the slack. I trod lightly down the path from my hut to the beach.

To the pile of sand, like a great misshapen wart on the rough and rugged skin of the beach.

The waves lapped at the shore. The tidal hush. I remembered what Xoff had said about the tides, about them washing up the creek bed to the temple.

The sack of coins had been too heavy, but the idol must have been swept away, jostled loose by the high tide, then dragged downstream by the low.

Here. To the sand pile. Or, rather, to this spot. And then the sand had . . .

Had moved to cover it? To protect it?

My feet brushed a path through the ring of offerings from the villagers, nudging aside cockles and reed-woven necklaces and seaweed garland. Hesitated just a moment before touching the pile. One of my rules of thievery: *Don't touch nothing you don't know won't touch back.* But I had to have it. It was *mine.* I stole it right and proper. I began to dig into the cold sand. It was like burrs in my skin. Should have brought a shovel.

But my hands served me well enough as I plowed through the pile, hurling fistfuls of sand behind me. Soon. I could feel it, calling to me. Soon . . .

There, in the hazy starlight, I saw the dull glimmer of stone. I felt a wash of relief. I had it again. I would be safe again.

"I told you, Da'an!"

With effort, I wrenched myself away from the hole I'd gouged out of the pile. A few yards away stood Xoff and Da'an.

"I knew he was up to something!" Xoff crowed. "I knew there was something off about him."

"You disguise it well," Da'an told me, almost sadly. "But to the trained ear, you sound like a city dweller . . ."

"I am from the city," I told them, my tone light. "Came here when I lost my wife to a gang of thugs." The lie came easily. I'd used variants of it before. "No harm in a man taking a walk on the beach."

"And digging in this sand pile?" Da'an asked, coming closer. "What exactly are you digging *for*, Gallric? Does it have anything to do with whatever you've got hidden in the old temple?"

I'm sure my face betrayed nothing—I've been shocked by the best and never let it show—but Xoff, lingering farther from the waterline, chimed in.

"You're up to *something* out here. We heard you moving floorboards around when we were upstairs."

Tell every truth you can afford.

Before Da'an could get to me, I reached into the hole and hauled out the idol, holding it aloft. "You're right. I was hiding this. But it wasn't there anymore."

> I HAD TO HAVE IT.
> IT WAS *MINE.*
> I STOLE IT RIGHT
> AND PROPER.

At the sight of the idol, Da'an stopped dead in her tracks and gasped. "Where did you get that?"

"It was in the temple," I told her, evading the truth about its original location. "It washed downstream."

"Put it down!" she shrieked, her eyes wide, her expression horrified. "Drop it where you stand!"

I glanced at it. The seaweed hair. The sharp teeth. The patina of green. For a moment, my vision went blurry, like sweat in your eyes, despite the bitter cold.

"It's just . . ." I blinked away the blurriness as I stared at the idol. It seemed to have changed.

It seemed older, and also cleaner.

"Have a care and put the damned thing down," Xoff said. He'd come closer, summoned by the fear in Da'an's voice. They were close to me now.

"It came here," Da'an said, each word trembling as it came out. "And it made the fishes leap. And the sand monument. And—"

"It just washed down here," I told her, gripping it tightly. "It was an accident."

"An accident?" Da'an yelled. "There are no accidents, you fool! This has happened just as they desired!"

They. The Drowned.

I wanted to laugh. I wanted to say I didn't believe.

But even Xoff looked ill as he stared at me. I'd been so sure that he was right all along, but now...

My skin prickled with sudden heat where I touched the idol.

I had to drop it.

But I couldn't drop it.

I had to.

I *wouldn't*.

Da'an rushed at me, then. I raised the idol to strike her with it, but in that moment, she tackled me, knocking me to the ground. The idol slipped from my hand as she bore me down.

I managed to slip from her grasp, rolling in the sand before popping up a few feet away. She was still down, looking for purchase, the sand tripping her when she tried to rise.

"Stay where you stand." Xoff was a ways away from me, but he had begun gesturing with his hands, sparks flitting around his fingertips.

I charged at him, grabbing his wrist and twisting as hard as I could, forcing him to stop.

He punched me in the side. A flare of pain erupted. Hadn't been punched in a long time; I'd lost my tolerance for the surprise of it.

I stumbled back and fell in the sand. Xoff loomed over me, but I lunged up and—

I froze in a half crouch at what I saw, not far away, just down the grade to the waterline.

> "THERE ARE NO ACCIDENTS, YOU FOOL! THIS HAS HAPPENED JUST AS THEY DESIRED!"

Da'an now held the idol, still down on her knees. But behind her...

Dark-shrouded shapes emerged from the night-black sea. They had the form of men and women, but their flesh was tattered, their clothing rags clotted with strands of seaweed. Their eyes glittered like chips of polished obsidian.

I tried to speak but could only find the air to gasp.

It was true. *They* were here. Da'an was right. Da'an had been right all along.

The sound of bells rang out, sour but clear on the night air. Some of the figures stepping out of the deep carried them, ringing them. The sound made Xoff turn away from me, staring down the beach.

"What...?" he whispered.

Before he could move, the figures were upon Da'an, who shouted out in terror. Xoff froze in place. *I froze in place.*

Behind me, I heard a murmur. Islanders had come to the sound of the bells. Half of the village, it seemed like, drawn by the ringing and the chiming.

"Go back!" I yelled. "Go back!"

They didn't listen. They stared, silent. Did they think these were their precious Druids? Or some punishment being visited on them by a demon of the deep?

Did they even care which?

At the waterline, four of the figures from the water held Da'an fast—two at her arms, one at her legs.

The fourth held her head steady in sea-slick hands, forcing her to look at the idol.

Xoff was whispering. Curses or prayers, I couldn't tell which. Either one seemed to make sense at the moment.

"Xoff!" Da'an cried in terror. "Xoff!"

It broke him from his reverie, and he stumble-ran down the sands to her. The things from the sea held her fast. They pushed her face closer to the idol.

Her scream stabbed my heart. I'd never heard such a cry from a human throat.

And still the bells chimed. And still the islanders came, shuffling their feet along the sand!

Da'an screamed again, her face closer to the idol. A sort of sickly light puddled in the air between her and the idol. As I watched, her eyes began to bleed. Something dark green and viscous wept from them.

Xoff stopped in his tracks.

Da'an's eyes drooled the green ichor. It dribbled in clotted rivulets down her cheeks, clung to the curve of her jaw, dripped onto her clothes and the sand. She hissed and spat and turned those horrible, horrible eyes to her companion.

"*NOW DO YOU BELIEVE?*" she cried, and laughed until her voice broke and became a grunting howl.

She never spoke again.

Xoff screamed and stumbled backward, flinging sand in every direction as he tried to flee. But the figures from the water were on him in a heartbeat, their slimy and dead hands strong upon him. Silent, they dragged his screaming form toward the idol.

Xoff began to keen in terror, high-pitched and childlike. More figures emerged from the water and scuttled up the sands like crabs toward the islanders.

But none approached me, though I stood within reach, just like the others. As I froze in place, still as my beloved idol who had caused all of this to happen, one of the creatures turned its head with slow purpose, staring up the slope of the beach at me. Its cracked lips parted, and it sizzed a long, sibilant syllable. Its eyes found mine, and I could not stare, but I could also not stop staring.

I thought perhaps its mouth twisted up into something like a smile, the joy of sharks and piranha. Sharp teeth bared in ecstasy. And it tilted its head as though to acknowledge.

As though . . .

I thought perhaps as though . . .

I thought perhaps as though to *thank me*.

I ran.

I ran from the beach. I ran to the docks. I flung myself bodily into the first boat I saw, cast off its line, and rowed with all my might. I rowed through the night, my breath hot and hard, puffing in clouds all around me. When morning's light glinted at the horizon, I took strength from the opening eye of the sun and heaved harder at my oars.

On land, I ran again, ignoring my body's exhaustion. I had left my stash behind, my life's work, my treasure, and I did not even realize it until two full days later, when I woke in a thicket, covered in ants and raccoon shit.

I thought of my stash no more. I brushed myself off, and then I ran more.

Farther, higher.

I ran until I came here, to the top of the mountain, to the farthest place from the sea I could find. Where the waves did not crash and there was no sand, no tides. I thought I'd run far enough—until I caught it the other night, a whiff of salt. And even now, I smell it still, as you smell it, the salt air that will soon go brackish and bleak.

They are coming, as Da'an foretold.

So I have to run again.

But here at the top of the world, there's nowhere left to run to.

The Tomb of Tal Rasha

BRIAN EVENSON

ILLUSTRATED BY
JOSH TALLMAN

I.

"I must ask again, are you certain?" said a voice behind him.

Tal Rasha stared at the binding stone that Tyrael had helped them shape and etch with runes of containment. Tal Rasha had captured Baal in the shard of the Amber Soulstone after a long and arduous battle; but the Horadrim knew the containment of the Prime Evil would be short-lived unless the shard was combined with a human. Within moments, Tal Rasha would be inextricably bound to the shard, and by extension to the very Prime Evil he and his brethren had sought so desperately to destroy.

The voice addressing Tal Rasha was that of Zoltun Kulle. He had asked this question first as Tyrael had led them through subterranean tunnels and into these burial chambers of long-dead kings. He had asked yet again when they had begun to shape the binding stone and forge the unbreakable chains. And now, before it was too late, he was asking a third time.

"I am certain," Tal Rasha said. And by saying it he found that he was. His whole life had been dedicated to justice and light. If he were to balk now, millions would die at Baal's hands, playthings to his greed for destruction. Better that one man should perish than the whole world suffer, even if that one man happened to be him.

As Tyrael directed the Horadrim in affixing the chains and in the chants that would make the binding eternal, Tal Rasha took a deep breath. This would be his last moment of peace before a half life of eternal struggle. He felt the manacles tighten around his wrists, felt his arms and legs stretch tight. He closed his eyes and uttered a silent prayer for the Eternal Light to give him strength to withstand the difficult path he had chosen. When he opened his eyes again, Tyrael was there, looming just before him, the glowing shard held delicately between his fingers.

"I am ready," said Tal Rasha.

Tyrael nodded once. "So be it," he said, and drove the shard deep into Tal Rasha's being.

The pain was enormous. Immediately he was writhing in agony, the fire in his chest searing and unrelenting as he felt his body being transformed into a prison for the terrible Baal. He cried out, gnashing his teeth, as his Horadrim brethren and Tyrael stood motionless before him, watching. *Help me!* a part of him wanted to say. *The pain is too great! I was wrong!*

He bit down on his tongue until his mouth was full of blood, his body shaking and rattling in the chains, the presence of Baal uncomfortable and menacing: so much love of destruction, and this—this agony! this evil!—would be his only companion for not mere days or weeks or months, but years and years. He felt Baal pushing at his mind and body, scouring for weaknesses, shaking the very foundations of his soul. His brothers slowly turned away and filed out. Then came the sound of the stone door grating closed and chanting from the other side as it was sealed with runes, and Tal Rasha was left all alone in the flickering light, writhing, wriggling, unable to catch his breath, hardly able to think, struggling to remember he was human.

Only, he wasn't alone, exactly.

Why have your brethren abandoned you? whispered Baal.

Tal Rasha tried not to listen.

Why have they left you behind? If they were truly your brothers, they would never have done so. My brothers and I, we look out for one another. True brothers do. Are your brothers so false?

"There was . . . no choice," said Tal Rasha, panting as he forced out the words.

There is always a choice. How is it, after all you have done to serve them, they allowed you to sacrifice yourself?

Tal Rasha could see Zoltun now in his mind's eye as he'd made the decision to sacrifice himself. Was that a flicker of satisfaction he glimpsed, before it was quickly hidden away? Had this been what Zoltun wanted all along?

Zoltun Kulle is hardly as pure as he allows you and the others to believe . . .

Tal Rasha groaned. "No," he said. "I won't . . . listen . . . to you!"

But whether he listened now or not it was too late: the idea was already planted in his mind. Why had Zoltun done nothing to try to stop him? He could remember the others, the horror and shock on their faces as they realized what their leader had agreed to do, but Zoltun's face had been blank, expressionless.

Hadn't it?

Or was this all wrong? Was he being forced to misremember in a way that—

Baal's voice resonated in his skull, disrupting his thoughts, sending them swirling away.

The others protested, but did he?

Did he? He was losing his footing again, seeing only Zoltun's cruel face as he stayed silent while the others tried to keep Tal Rasha from taking the burden upon himself. True, he had never asked Tal Rasha to offer up his own life, but he had never volunteered himself either. Zoltun had known that if he waited long enough, if he directed him just enough, Tal Rasha would take the burden upon himself, just as he had desired . . .

But wait, no, was he remembering it correctly? It didn't seem right, but surely it had just happened. Surely it was fresh in his mind . . .

That demonic voice again, more insistent now: *Zoltun Kulle came up with the accursed idea! He could have volunteered himself at any time. He never did! He wanted you to leave so that he would become the head of the Order. This was all an elaborate ploy to take your place.*

No, it wasn't true! It couldn't be! It was not Zoltun Kulle he should doubt but this whispering, lying voice: Baal.

"Begone, demon!" he cried. "I command thee, depart!"

For a moment there was silence in his head, no whispering, no other voice, though his body continued to contort and struggle. And then, starting low and rising, he heard Baal's awful laughter.

You fool! said Baal. *I cannot be banished or dismissed. Your very body is the place of my banishment! Our fates are bound together now. You cannot rid yourself of me.* He chuckled again, malicious. His voice, when he spoke again, was low and deadly. *Or perhaps I should say, you cannot escape me . . .*

The demon stretched, and Tal Rasha felt needles within his skin as the demon again tested the bounds of his prison. He cried out, and his mouth filled with blood. His vision grew blurred and dark. He was panting, exhausted.

Would that I could simply destroy you, said Baal, *that I could trample your body into a slick of blood and bring about your annihilation as I have done with so many. I am not well disposed to patience, particularly when I have no choice.*

And now, even with his eyes closed, Tal Rasha felt that he could see Baal's cruel mien staring back at him out of the darkness.

I cannot destroy you all at once, Baal said, *and so I will destroy you bit by bit. I will take one part of your mind and crush it, then another, then another, until you are reduced to nothing. Until you are less than nothing, an empty shell. And then I will crack you open and crawl out of you.*

Tal Rasha opened his eyes, but Baal's face still remained, marring his vision like a smear. *What have I condemned myself to?* he asked himself, but he already knew. Despite his love of the Light, despite his countless deeds upholding justice, in order to save the world he had sentenced himself to a living hell. He was filled with infinite regret, a regret that, he knew, was likely to last forever.

But haven't I already been here forever?

> TAL RASHA OPENED HIS EYES, BUT BAAL'S FACE STILL REMAINED, MARRING HIS VISION LIKE A SMEAR.

As suddenly as the vision had begun—for indeed a vision was what it had been, he could see that now—it fizzled away. *None of this just happened.* By Tal Rasha's estimation, he had already been suffering for a few years. But what was a mere handful of years in the face of eternity?

He looked down and saw his struggling body, emaciated and barely human. He felt the eternal hunger that had been with him for nearly as long as he could remember, the thirst that left him forever parched and always just a hairsbreadth shy of death. His body struggled, yanking at its bonds. It both was and wasn't his body now, he knew, and he both was and wasn't the one struggling.

In a flash, he knew that the scene with Zoltun had been fed to him by Baal, a subtle reworking of what had actually happened, with Baal keeping nearly everything the same while nevertheless introducing shades of doubt and fear, making him mistrust himself and his brethren—to weaken Tal Rasha's mind even further and break him apart piece by piece, just as the Lord of Destruction had promised to do.

But at least this time, Tal Rasha had seen through it.

"You cannot . . . fool me . . . with your illusions, demon!"

And yet I have fooled you with this same illusion time and time again, mage. Each time it takes you a little longer to understand that it is an illusion. Your mind is crumbling. And soon it shall be reduced to ash, and I will be free.

No, thought Tal Rasha, *you're lying.* But deep inside him he knew it was true, that he had been through this before and yet had forgotten.

Baal laughed. *Another piece of you gone! There you go, grain by grain, dispersed into nothingness. You Horadrim with your so-called love of justice, believing that knowledge will be enough to save you. How quaint! Just because you recognize what is happening to you doesn't mean that you can prevent it from happening . . .*

II.

He opened his eyes onto darkness, silence. It took a moment for him to realize where he was. *What a terrible dream,* he thought. The light of the waning crescent moon through his cell window was so dim that he could see almost nothing at all. He groped along the floor beside his pallet until he found the earthenware cup and raised it to his lips, drinking the tepid water. But, strangely enough, as soon as he'd drunk the water and set the cup down, he felt thirsty again.

What time was it? Early, no doubt, too early to be getting up, but after such a dream how could he sleep? No, better to rise and light a candle and get to work. He had his history to record, the true story of how he had been chosen by Tyrael to be the leader of the Horadrim, how he had sacrificed himself to save the world, and how, miraculously, his life had been returned to him, his glory had been returned to him, so that now he was again among the Horadrim, the defenders of truth and light, and dedicated to a monastic life of contemplation and wisdom.

He rose from his pallet once more and slipped on his robe, then fumbled through the darkness, hands outstretched, until his fingers touched the back of his chair.

He settled onto it and pulled it closer to the crude wooden table that served him as a desk, then cast his hands carefully over its surface, past the ever-present stack of books, brushing the feathered ends of the quills, until he found the candle, it sides stippled with wax drippings.

He mumbled a simple spell, and it sprang alight. He arranged a blank half-sheet of foolscap before him. Choosing a quill from the cup that held them, he dipped the pen in ink and began to write.

I found myself, he wrote, *in the depths. I was breaking but not yet broken. I clung to what I had learned, to the truths that Tyrael had revealed to me, and hoped that the bedrock of this great knowledge would be enough to allow me to survive until my fellow Horadrim figured out a way to rescue my body, a way to substitute something else as a prison for Baal. Surely Tyrael would find some means to bring the shards of the Amber Soulstone back together, or perhaps the means to carve another prison from what remained of the Worldstone. I had to continue to hope, I knew. And I must not, above all, give way to despair.*

Reaching the end of the page he drew back, waiting for the ink to dry before he added it to the stack of finished pages at his elbow. He blew lightly on the words to facilitate this, but as he did so, the letters seemed to twist and move, dancing madly in the candle's flame. He shook his head, but the words were still moving, little rivulets of ink darting across the page. Frowning, he peered closer, rereading what he had written.

Only a few years into his captivity, Tor'Baalos, Lord of Destruction, esteemed spawn of one of the primary heads of Tathamet, had broken the will of the meddlesome mage. The once proud Tal Rasha had become a shadow of his former self, his mind reduced to a residue of impulses that Baal could shape as putty to his will. However, Tyrael's magic could not yet be defeated. Though Tal Rasha's heart had become weakened and diseased, it, combined with the shard, still held Baal imprisoned. And yet it was his jailer who suffered more than Baal himself. For each year he kept Baal imprisoned, it felt as though Tal Rasha suffered in the Burning Hells for a thousand years. Soon Tal Rasha's mind would be gone, and his body would be entirely subject to Baal's will. All the great Baal would have to do was to be patient.

But patience did not come easily to Baal. Fortunately, he had his jailer upon which to take out his frustrations.

Tal Rasha felt his blood grow chill. He reached for the page to tear it in two, but as he did he saw that his reaching hand was dark red and scaly, and terminated in sharp gray claws. He lifted it to his face and stared at it, then pushed back the sleeve of his robe. There, too, the skin was red and scaled. He reached up to his face, felt the way his mouth puckered strangely, fingered the tips of the long fangs. His hand traveled upward, touched the curled horns that jutted from the crown of his head.

"No!" he said aloud. "It can't be!"

He was imagining things. This couldn't be happening. But then again, how had he escaped? Was that not impossible as well? Unless, perhaps, he had sold his soul and ended up giving in to darkness. Had it gone so far? Was this why he had become a demon?

At first, no one responded to his pounding at the locked door. And then, finally, as he paused to catch his breath between shouts, he heard, at a distance, a door opening and shutting.

"Hello?" he called. "Please, help me!"

Nobody answered. After a time, he heard the sound of footsteps drawing nearer, then nearer still, finally stopping just outside his door.

"Who is it?" he asked. "Open this door at once!"

> HE SAW THAT HIS REACHING HAND WAS DARK RED AND SCALY, AND TERMINATED IN SHARP GRAY CLAWS.

"I will not open the door," said a voice that he recognized as Zoltun Kulle's. His second-in-command, the very person who he had feared would take over leadership of the Order when he had been left alone to struggle with Baal in the tomb. His betrayer!

"I command it!" Tal Rasha said, and waited. But still the door did not open.

At last, Zoltun spoke, his voice tired, exhausted, as if this was a conversation he had had far too many times.

"We have done what we can for you," said Zoltun. "We have, as requested, provided you with writing implements so that you can record all that has happened to you. We have given you every comfort possible. We have made of your necessary solitude a life of contemplation. Perhaps one day you may be released, once we know that we can trust you again."

Tal Rasha felt rage well up within him. How could those who had once served him have the appalling temerity to believe they could control him so! He pounded again on the door.

"Release me!" he cried. "Cure me of this curse!"

From the other side of the door, Zoltun's voice remained calm. "Even if I so desired, I could not. The door has been meticulously bound shut. It would take all the Horadrim working together to remove the runes of binding. As for your curse, you brought it upon yourself. Return to your desk. Record your history, share your wisdom with us, slide the papers out under the door. We will gather them, read them, consult among ourselves. Perhaps, one day, when the time is right, we will release you."

"This is unjust," said Tal Rasha. "By holding me you are breaking your vow to serve justice!"

But Zoltun said nothing in response. As Tal Rasha listened, he heard footsteps move slowly away, and then, finally, in the distance, the sound of a door shutting.

Not knowing what else to do, he returned to his desk. He examined his scaly hand. How had this come to happen? He reached for a quill, and when he picked one up it became engulfed in flame, but it only felt comfortably warm in his hand. *Just like home,* he thought, almost without realizing what that implied. *Shall I try again?* he wondered, and then, because he did not know what, if anything, else he could do, he lifted the pen and began to write.

I am not sure what has happened to me, he wrote with the burning pen. The air filled with a pungent odor, and he realized that he was writing not on paper but on parchment, made from the skin of an animal. Or rather, he was sure, though he was not sure how he was sure, not an animal, but the skin of a human. *A perfect recording surface for a demon such as myself,* he thought.

Is this real? he wrote. *Am I still dreaming?* He found himself staring out the window. It was, he saw, still dark outside—it was impossible to see anything, except that same sliver of moon. Once morning came, perhaps he could leap from the window and escape that way. With his free hand he reached toward the opening, but before he could cross its surface a bluish fire began to play over it, and he found he could not touch it. Of course. The Horadrim were careful and efficient; they would have left nothing to chance.

A scratching sound distracted him. He glanced down and saw that while he had been lost in thought his clawed hand had been idly doodling. There was a face there now, crudely drawn but nonetheless a face. He peered at it, looking at it more closely. It looked familiar. He stared, and then by impulse began to redraw a few lines, reconnect others, all to the accompaniment of the smell of burning flesh. He still couldn't quite place the face until, suddenly, abruptly he could: it was the face of Tal Rasha.

That's my face, he realized with a start. *That's who I really am.* He reached up and touched his head and found the horns were no longer there. He looked back at the drawing, but that was gone too. The whole desk was gone, and the cell, too, was fading around him. All that remained was the flickering light of the candle . . .

But it was not from a candle any longer. It was the flickering light that illuminated the tomb. He was back where he had always been, bound to the stone, twisting and turning in endless combat with Baal. But he knew where he was, knew who he was. He had not broken—yet.

Baal gave a low chuckle.

"You have failed . . . to break me . . . again," panted Tal Rasha.

Baal hissed. *I am hollowing you out from the inside. With every failure I come closer to succeeding. With every success, you come closer to your final failure.*

"You are a . . . worthy opponent," Tal Rasha said, "but I shall . . . continue to triumph."

You, on the other hand, said Baal, *are a fool and a waste of my time.*

III.

How many years had it been? One? Two? A decade? A century? He did not know. Nor did he know how much longer he could hold out. An impossible task, it turned out, resisting a Prime Evil.

Baal was becoming more inventive, manipulating and pushing his mind more and

more effectively, making him more malleable. In the end, he knew, he would only be a hollow version of what he had once been, not even close to human. He was already well on the way there. The last vision had been as bad as any; each time Baal altered his reality, the demon watched carefully for what upset Tal Rasha the most, made careful note of it, and amplified it in whatever came next.

You will never be free, he told himself. *In the end, you will collapse. But even once you do, the binding will still hold; he will still be imprisoned within you. You will still have saved the world.*

If you are to give in eventually, came Baal's voice from within his head, *why not give in now?*

Why not *give in now?* he wondered. It would bring the torture to a stop. His body tensed and contorted, squirmed, but it had been happening for so long, so many years now, that he almost no longer noticed it, the pain a constant scream that never dissipated, his vocal cords long gone raw—his hunger perpetual, his thirst too. A true hell.

Why not give in? Why not end it?

But would it really end? Could he be sure? Once he gave in, perhaps it would simply allow Baal to make things worse.

He writhed, breathed through his teeth. He bit his tongue, but whatever blood had been in him was mostly dried up; it came torpidly, and didn't last long.

How much longer can I survive?

Something was nagging at him. What was it? Something *felt* different. Something *was* different. And then he realized: one of his hands was no longer restrained. The chain that bound it had somehow come loose.

It was impossible.

And yet . . .

No, not impossible, just improbable. There were, he realized, circumstances where it might just be possible. A syllable mispronounced or skipped when the binding spell was uttered, perhaps by only one of the Horadrim, not enough to be noticed in the chorus of voices by Tyrael, but just enough to introduce a subtle flaw, a weakness that over time would cause the rune to slowly fail.

Yes, it was just possible. Perhaps that, combined with his increasingly diminished physical body, had been enough to allow him to slip free of one of his chains even while the others remained implacably in place. His hand could now reach out and grab the shard that was in his chest. Could even tug it out, if he so chose.

How tempting that was! To be free of this torment once and for all, to allow his body, so long tortured, to rest, perhaps even to die . . . Hadn't he suffered enough? How could any mortal be asked to endure torment such as this?

And yet, he had promised to save the world. He had sacrificed himself, willingly. If he were to go back on this promise, all that he had sacrificed would have been for naught.

No, he couldn't give up. And now he had added one more burden to those already heaped upon him: he must not let Baal know that his arm was unchained, must not in fact think about it at all. If he did, Baal would wrest control of Tal Rasha's own hand, use it to tug the golden shard free and release him from his captor.

He felt despair welling up in him. How long could he keep his secret? One slip and it was over. One slip, and he would betray the world.

Something is different, Baal thought. The arrogant mage, the worm, had become cagey. The vermin was hiding something. Amusing that he thought he could keep it a secret from *him*, Tor'Baalos, who had millennia of interactions with demons and angels and humans to tell him when someone was trying to deceive him.

Baal was sick of being trapped here, with this uptight mage with his *principles* and his *values*, who had somehow convinced himself that the Sanctuary would be a better world if it stayed always the same, stagnant, unchanging. *Bah,* sneered Baal. What fun was that? And what fun was this mage? Both of them knew that he couldn't hold out forever—and Baal knew too that someday, something would change, that the idea that he could be bound for eternity in a place like this was part and parcel of the naïve belief that things wouldn't change. But things *did* change. And he *would* get out. And once he was out, he would pop this arrogant little mage's head like a grape. Then he would devastate this world and everything in it, kill everything he saw, growing stronger with each act of slaughter. He had a lot of mayhem to catch up on.

But what was different now? What was this runt hiding from him? He worked his way into the man's puny mind and found him thinking obsessively about the fact that he was *trapped* here, that there was no escape. That was nothing new—the mage had been playing intermittently with this one putrid thought for years and years now, turning it this way and that, examining it from every angle—but something about it this time gave Baal pause. Shortly, he realized what it was: Tal Rasha never thought with such obsession about his plight. He thought about it, true, but not obsessively. What had shifted?

And then it occurred to Baal: *He was trying not to think about something else.*

He pushed farther in. The man's mind was so easy to penetrate, its hallways regular and straight and *boring*, nothing dynamic here. That Tyrael had ever thought of this man as a worthy vessel to contain him was incredible to Baal. But then again, the idiot archangel had always underestimated him and his brothers and would no doubt continue to do so.

> BAAL WAS SICK OF BEING TRAPPED HERE, WITH THIS UPTIGHT MAGE WITH HIS *PRINCIPLES* AND HIS *VALUES*.

He pushed his way through Tal Rasha's mind, looking for dark corners, places where things might be hidden. There were one or two things, moments from his childhood that he kept hidden, perhaps even from himself. Nothing of real consequence, but things Baal filed away as fodder for potential inclusion in future visions.

And then, suddenly, there it was, a newly patched wall, so to speak, mortar still damp. So *obvious*, hidden in plain sight. It was always a pleasure to make a wall collapse. He prodded on it with his forelegs, and it crumbled inward, and there it was.

At first Baal couldn't believe it, but as he sorted through Tal Rasha's reasoning, slowly drawing it out of the man bit by painful bit, he began to believe that, yes, it was possible. The fools! They couldn't even cast a binding spell correctly! And yes, Tal Rasha's worries were correct: *he* still couldn't escape from the binding, but Baal now could. All he needed was to take control of Tal Rasha's hand and . . .

But the mage proved remarkably resistant. He had clearly been preparing for this eventuality for some time. How infuriating! If he was out of this prison, Baal would simply tear the brat's head from his shoulders and be done with him. They struggled back and forth, with Baal doing all he could to assert his will, until, finally, exhausted, Tal Rasha's guard momentarily slipped.

It was all Baal needed.

He rushed in and took control of the hand, and a moment later it had closed around the shard that Tyrael had jammed deep within Tal Rasha's flesh. Tal Rasha screamed and fought to regain control, but it was already too late. The shard had already been withdrawn and cast aside.

Baal was free.

It was exhilarating, being released after all these years! He rushed for the exit. Surely there was some sort of alarm trigger, which would mean that it was only a matter of time before that busybody Tyrael arrived. Hearing behind him the anguished cries of the collapsed and helpless Tal Rasha, Baal nearly doubled back to finish him off, but even he knew that would be reckless. He had to flee while he still had the chance.

"Another day, Tal Rasha!" Baal cried, cackling with glee. He would find his brothers, and together they would come back and make short work first of Tal Rasha and then of the High Heavens. There would be time enough to track down this ruined husk of a man. For now, let him stay bound to the stone, dying his slow and painful death.

> IF HE WAS OUT OF THIS PRISON, BAAL WOULD SIMPLY TEAR THE BRAT'S HEAD FROM HIS SHOULDERS.

Baal had to use all his strength to move the stone that blocked the tomb. *Funny*, he thought, *I would have thought they would have bound this in place as well.* He remembered that from the nightmare he had given Tal Rasha a few years before, but perhaps that detail had been his own addition to the story: he had changed so many small details in the visions he had manufactured that it was sometimes hard to remember what had been real.

The block rolled away, grinding against the stone, and he stepped into the tunnel beyond. He rushed through it, deserted as it was. He passed other tombs, and now he could hear behind him the sound of Tyrael rising, beckoning after him, searching for him. A good thing that Baal hadn't indulged himself and gone back to slaughter Tal Rasha—if he had, he'd be in the heat of battle right now.

And suddenly, there it was: the exit to the outside world. Baal swung the double doors open and rushed out the other side . . .

. . . only to find the inside of the same tomb.

> IT WAS EXHILARATING, BEING RELEASED AFTER ALL THESE YEARS!

What? There was no outside. How could this be? What sort of curse was this?

And where was Tyrael? He could no longer hear the sounds of the archangel's imminent arrival.

He pushed through the doors again and found himself outside at last, but surrounded by . . . what could those be? Cows? But bipedal and carrying polearms? What fresh hell was this? They rushed forward, mooing at him, and with a flick of his forelegs he sent a wave of ice to mow them down. They were nothing, easily defeated, and yet they kept coming, and coming, and coming.

Troubled, he stepped back through the doors to gather himself and think, and found himself in the tomb again. When, after a moment, he opened the doors again, he found himself looking out upon the inverse mirror of the tomb. Once again, there was no outside.

Did I miss my chance?

Which way should I go? Back the way I came, or into its mirror image?

He hesitated. It was not like the Lord of Destruction to hesitate, and yet he did. And then he plunged into the mirror image of the tomb.

Slowly, with increasing dread, he crept back the way he had come, following the same path but in reverse, into a backward version of the world.

He came at last to the rock he had rolled aside. He hesitated there, not sure that he wanted to see what was on the other side, but, at last, not knowing what else to do, he passed through.

There, on the other side, still perfectly chained, still impeccably attached to the binding stone, was Tal Rasha.

The shard was still anchored deep within his flesh. His body was still contorted in agony as his features flickered back and forth between his own human face and the monstrous face of Baal.

Baal howled with frustration. To have been made to think that he was free when he had never been free at all! To be bested, he, by a mere mortal, even if only for a few moments. What would his brothers say if they could bear witness to what had happened?

And upon thinking that, he found himself not standing observing Tal Rasha, but back within the crystal, back within Tal Rasha, his fleshy prison.

Trapped.

Despite his pain, despite his state of perpetual agony, Tal Rasha smiled. He had, for once, given Baal some of his own medicine. The victory was pyrrhic and fleeting, but he had managed to preserve a tiny piece of himself. Perhaps he could hold on to sanity for a little longer after all.

But then, within him, Baal began to rage. His smile quickly extinguished, Tal Rasha began to scream with pain.

When the Dark Seeps In

DELILAH S. DAWSON

ILLUSTRATED BY
ZOLTAN BOROS

I.

It was raining the day Timeth learned how to say goodbye.

He was only four, and before that, he hadn't had much use for the word. It was just Mother, Father, and his older brother, Patrok, and not one of them strayed too far from the little thatched cottage, the snug barn, and the neat garden, all contained within a tumbledown rock wall in a lonely corner of Scosglen. Sometimes Mother or Father went out the wooden gate to visit the neighboring small village over the hill, and Father often went hunting in the forest, but they were always back before nightfall with lively things to talk about and good things to eat.

Well—usually. Not in the past few weeks. Timeth's belly grumbled a lot more, lately.

"Say goodbye, little love. Patrok is going to meet the Druids," Mother said, holding Timeth up so he could look his older brother in the eye. Patrok was twelve, an unimaginably old age, and he was going off all on his lonesome with just a ragged brown cloak and some bread tied up in a kerchief.

"What's a Druid?" Timeth asked.

Mother and Father shared a glance, turning to their eldest.

"Those who speak to the winds and the beasts and the forest," Patrok answered for them. "Legend says they are wise and have many great powers. They will surely help us." He frowned as he looked around the farm, but then he smiled at Timeth. "Plus, with me gone, that's more for you to eat!" He tickled Timeth, and Timeth laughed and forgot all the frowning and worried looks passing between Mother and Father.

"Back for supper?" Timeth asked, for no one had ever been gone overnight before.

"I'll be gone a long time," Patrok told him.

"But I'll always be thinking about you and looking out for you, even if we're far apart."

Timeth leaned out of his mother's arms, and Patrok caught him and nuzzled his head. When Mother pulled Timeth away again, he clung to his brother, tears filling his eyes.

"No, Patty!" he screeched. "Stay!"

Patrok backed up, one step after the other, his eyes pleading for understanding.

"It's for the best, Tim," he said with a sniffle. "Take care of Mother and Father?"

"No!" Timeth wailed, and then Patrok turned and ran through the gate, nearly tripping over his own feet in Father's old boots.

Timeth tried to run after Patrok, but Mother caught him easily and swung him up into her arms and carried him inside and shut the door, securing the big lock that was too high for him to reach. Timeth cried until he collapsed, and then she fed him his mush and tucked him up in his little trundle bed.

But he was too upset to sleep, and he heard Mother and Father murmuring in the big bed from the corner of the room.

"How will he find the way?" Mother asked. "There are rumors in the village—"

"Fie on the village," Father said angrily. "What do they know? Haven't seen a Druid in three generations. The tall tales grow bigger every year. The forests of Scosglen belong to the Druids. If they want him, he'll be found."

"And if not?" Oh, how Mother's voice wobbled!

"If not, we'll never know, will we? There's no future for the boy here. The crops dwindle, the cow's milk has dried up, the chickens aren't laying. When I go hunting, the beasts are hard to find, and sometimes I come across one that's . . . twisted. Wrong." Mother sounded like she might be crying now, but the bed creaked as Father drew her close. "Look, love. Patrok is a clever lad. If the Druids take him in, he has a chance at a better life. That's all we can ever hope for."

"And what of the wee lad?" Mother whispered, but Timeth heard it and wondered if she was talking about him.

"If things get worse, when he's twelve, we'll send him out too." Father sighed. "Patrok was right. One less mouth to feed. Methinks we'll soon appreciate that."

Timeth fell asleep to the sound of his mother's soft sobs and his father's murmured promises. He dreamed of a small boy in a big, dark forest, running down a path with no beginning and no end.

II.

Eight Years Later

It was a good thing Timeth had learned to say goodbye that day when Patrok left for the forests, because the goodbyes came hard and fast as he grew up.

First Alesha the farm cat was found nearly inside out.

Then the milk cow just fell over one day, light as a dandelion puff, as if she'd been drained of her milk and blood, both.

Father brought home a brindle dog to help protect the property, but it ran away and was never seen again.

Grandmother and Grandfather, who lived near the village center, died in quick succession, maybe from being old and maybe from something else—no one seemed to know.

"The dark just keeps seeping in," Mother would sometimes say, and Father would shush her, but he never disagreed.

When Timeth was ten, Father went out hunting one day and didn't return. Mother went to look for him, and Uncle Joren came down to help her search, but no matter how far they roamed with their lanterns, calling his name, they never found hide nor hair of him. Timeth didn't know which would've been worse—the certainty of knowing his father had been killed, or learning he'd left them to venture out alone in search of someplace better.

> **WHEN TIMETH WAS TEN, FATHER WENT OUT HUNTING ONE DAY AND DIDN'T RETURN.**

Finally, worst of all, Mother died when Timeth was nearly twelve. He awoke at dawn to find her in her rocking chair by the fire, her skin gone gray and sunken. She'd faded away steadily after Father disappeared, insubstantial as a ghost, and even though she tried to hide it with extra shawls, Timeth knew she'd been denying herself food so that he would have enough.

At least he'd let her kiss his forehead the night before, for all that he felt too old for such things. Her lips had felt like cobwebs.

That morning, Timeth buried Mother out behind the barn, and he was surprised at what hard work it was, digging a grave. Standing over her, he felt like part of his soul had floated off without him, and although he knew he should say something, he didn't know what.

"Rest in peace, Mother," he managed—but felt that it was insufficient.

Perhaps he should've gone to the neighboring village, should've let Uncle Joren and what little family was left know what had happened. But in the last few years, Uncle Joren had stopped coming, and Mother had stopped going, making Timeth promise he wouldn't walk the path over the hill. The last time she'd gone, she'd been chased by . . . something. She wouldn't say what it was, but she never went over the hill again, and Timeth planned on keeping his promise.

That day, Timeth drew water from the well and weeded the gardens and pulled up one puny little carrot. He checked his snares and the fish trap and brought home a scrawny rabbit and a few finger-size fish. He swept the cottage floor and—

Fell to his knees, crying.

He was all that was left, and he was alone.

First Patrok, then Father, then Mother.

With each loss, the light and joy had been sucked out of his life until he couldn't remember the last time the sun had truly shone on his face. Sometimes he thought perhaps Patrok had never existed, that he was just a dream from a better time. Whenever he'd asked Mother and Father about Patrok, they'd changed the subject. The only sign that Patrok had ever truly existed was a little carved figure that maybe resembled a spotted dog in the right light. Timeth thought he remembered Patrok giving it to him, but then again, such a thing could've come from anywhere.

Later that day, Timeth stood over Mother's grave at sunset, a posy of ragged dandelions in his fist. He'd tied two sticks together to make a rough cross, but it still didn't seem like enough.

"Mother," he murmured, falling to his knees in the freshly turned dirt. "You can't be gone. I can't do this alone. I need help. The world is too hard." He looked up at the sky, at the birds wheeling overhead. "Help me!" he screamed.

The birds flapped away, cawing harshly. Embarrassed by his outburst, Timeth stood and dusted off his knees. He left the posy in the dirt and went inside before darkness fell.

III.

The next two years all ran together, dreary and gray, the sun hidden by oppressive clouds from dawn to dusk. Timeth went through the motions of his daily life but often found himself standing over Mother's grave as if he were half-asleep. Each night, he secured the big lock on the door. When he was young, it had seemed impossibly high, but now he could reach it easily. With the door shut, the cottage was snug and warm, and sleep was a welcome oblivion. He no longer rose with the sun. He ate little. Time had lost all meaning.

And then one morning, Timeth was awakened by an odd noise. He sat up, blinking his dreams away, uncertain how to proceed. In all his fourteen years, no one had ever come knocking at the cottage door.

He slid out of bed and picked up the big kitchen knife he kept sharp for cleaning fish. There was no way to see who might be outside, nor was there another exit to the cottage, unless he opened the shutters that had always remained firmly locked over the windows at Mother's request. It was almost entirely dark within, but the light that shone through the cracks glowed like molten gold.

"Hello?" Timeth barked.

"Good morning," the voice replied—a fine, mellow voice, definitely not what Timeth was expecting.

"What do you want?"

"It's good that you are distrustful," said the voice, sounding very reasonable. "We live in dangerous times. Are you the man of the house?"

"No," Timeth lied. "There are several of us in here, all armed to the teeth."

The voice chuckled. "Courage. I like that. Will you open the door?"

"What, so you can rob me?" Timeth shouted. "There's nothing left to take."

"Has it truly gotten so bad?" the voice asked, sounding genuinely concerned.

"It could not be worse," Timeth admitted, softening just a bit, because what did he have to lose by telling the truth?

"Then it's good that I've come," the voice said. "For I'm your brother, Patrok, and it just so happens I crossed paths with a young hart on my way here. It should feed us both for a while."

The breath caught in Timeth's throat. It was simply too good to be true.

"Patrok has been gone for ten years," he said. "Prove that you are he."

A fond sigh carried through the door. "The day I left, I wore Father's old boots. They were too big. I ran away so you wouldn't see me cry. I wanted you to think me brave."

"Anyone might guess that." Timeth dashed tears out of his eyes. "I need more proof."

"I carved a little dog for you when you were small," the voice said softly. "Not particularly well. I sliced my thumb and told you the bloodstain was a spot, that it was a spotted dog."

Knife still in his hand, hardly daring to hope, Timeth unlatched the door and let it swing inward. There, framed by the morning sun, was a big man, taller even than Father had been. Over a long green robe he wore layered gray pelts that accentuated his wide shoulders, and his long golden hair was braided back with beads and bits of bone. He had blue tattoos tracing up his forearms, and in one hand he held an imposing staff of twisted wood topped with a glittering crystal.

In the other hand, he held out a carving—a dog that actually looked like a dog.

"I got better," he said with a wry smile.

A smile that Timeth knew immediately.

He threw himself into his brother's arms, and when they pulled out of the hug, Timeth saw that springtime had arrived along with his visitor. The garden was full of green, the trees were unfurling their leaves and buds, and the birds were back, singing in the boughs.

And true to his word, a large, plump stag lay dead at Patrok's feet.

"Did you really find the Druids?" Timeth asked, now breathless with excitement.

Patrok chuckled and put a hand on his brother's shoulder. "I did."

"Are . . . are you a Druid now?"

"I am. And so might you be, one day, if you wish it." A golden amulet on Patrok's chest briefly glowed, and then he was scooping up the heavy deer as if it were nothing, heading for the barn. "Come help me clean him, and I'll tell you more."

> A GOLDEN AMULET ON PATROK'S CHEST BRIEFLY GLOWED, AND THEN HE WAS SCOOPING UP THE HEAVY DEER.

Timeth spent the rest of the day following Patrok, asking a million questions. Patrok did his best to answer what he could, although even he couldn't explain why the realm was falling to lawlessness and corruption, and why there were twisted beasts haunting the forest.

When Timeth asked him why he'd returned, Patrok looked up into the trees overhead and said only, "The birds talk." When Timeth asked him what that meant, he stopped what he was doing and looked his younger brother in the eyes. "Listen. It's no longer safe for you to go beyond the stone wall, especially not toward the village. Promise me you'll stay within, and I'll take care of the hunting and fishing. Together, we'll see this place flourish again, just as Mother and Father wished. Do you promise?"

"I . . . I suppose so." Timeth's brow drew down. "But I've been going beyond the wall ever since Father died. I brought home meat and fish for Mother. I'm strong. Why is it dangerous for me but fine for you?"

"It's dangerous for everyone," Patrok allowed. He pulled back his cloak to show the axe and dagger on his belt, then turned to show the crossbow and quiver on his back. "But I've been trained. I . . . sense things. I know what's out there, and I know how to fight it." He grinned. "Aren't younger brothers supposed to be lazy and argue for *less* chores, not more?"

Timeth wanted to insist that he was perfectly capable, but . . . well, he *was* scared of the world beyond. Just last week he'd found a two-headed baby rabbit, dead in the grass. And one time he'd been chased by a horrible thing, all quills and hisses, that had scratched at the garden gate after he'd thrown it shut. He couldn't forget Mother's whispered words about the dark seeping in. It was scary out there, but he didn't want Patrok to think he was weak.

Even if he *was* weak.

Living off gruel and cabbage would do that to a lad.

> ONE TIME HE'D BEEN CHASED BY A HORRIBLE THING, ALL QUILLS AND HISSES, THAT HAD SCRATCHED AT THE GARDEN GATE.

That night they dined on roast venison, made tender and succulent with herbs Patrok carried in his sporran. Timeth ate until his stomach bulged. He couldn't remember the last time he'd felt full. As they ate, Patrok asked him question after question, trying to fill in all the time that he'd lost. Hearing about Father, he frowned and leaned back. Hearing about Mother, he let loose a single tear. Finally, Patrok stood and yawned, his knuckles scraping the thatch of the ceiling.

"You can take the bed," Timeth offered, but Patrok only smiled.

"I've been sleeping on the ground for years. You take it."

When he'd banked the fire and locked the door, Patrok rearranged his cloak like a blanket and settled in, lying down right there in the entryway.

"It's warmer by the fire," Timeth said. "I know there's a draft."

But Patrok didn't move. He played with the knife from his belt, the sharpened metal glinting in the darkness. "I've slept in worse places."

It took a long time for Timeth to fall asleep. He was glad to see his older brother returned—overjoyed, really—but he was full of confusing emotions. Guilt that Mother had died on his watch. Shame over his father's abandonment. An aching sense of loss, to have spent most of his life starving and frightened, when the presence of his older brother might've been a balm. So many good memories they'd never made, and all the while his brother was somewhere far away, learning new things.

"What are the Druids like?" Timeth asked.

"They are everything the legends say, and yet more. Warriors and poet-kings, fierce fighters and spiritual seekers, raucous drinkers and solemn stoics. They told me it's possible our family is descended from—" He chuckled. "Well, that's a topic for another day. I traveled a long way to get here, and I reckon I'll sleep like a bear tonight. Good night, Tim." He rolled over, turning to face the door.

Timeth thought about what Patrok had said, how he'd described the Druids as a whole, but not as individuals, not as men. He didn't know anything more than before he'd asked. Patrok was good at that—answering questions in a way that left one with only more questions. Timeth trusted his brother, and yet . . . he felt a little uneasy around him. But with his full belly and the fire's warmth, sleep soon claimed him despite his doubts.

When he awoke the next morning, Patrok was gone, and Timeth momentarily thought it had all been a dream—except that the new dog carving was beside him on the pillow and some cold venison was laid out on the table for him, along with a little cress and fresh water from the well. The door was unlocked, but when he poked his head outside, he didn't see Patrok. The sun was still shining, and spring ran riot over the yard and garden. Everything was bright green, flowers already heavy-headed and blossoms dripping from the trees. Timeth had only planted the carrots, potatoes, and onions a few days ago, and yet their tops were verdant and knee-tall. He heard whistling, and Patrok pushed through the wooden gate in the stone wall, carrying a fish as long as his arm.

"You've kept the fish traps well, little brother!" he called. "Even with this fine fellow thrashing about, the trap held!"

Timeth gawped at the fish. "I haven't seen one that big in my entire life," he said. "Not even when Father would fish with worms."

Patrok just shrugged. "They migrate to spawn. It's just that time of year."

But it bothered Timeth a bit, that Patrok had such luck about him.

"Is this Druid magic?" Timeth asked. "First the stag, now the fish?"

Patrok regarded him coolly. "Is it magic, to know where the best mushrooms grow, year after year? Is it magic, to select the best bull to breed with your heifer?"

"I haven't seen a fish longer than my hand in any of those traps in six years, so if you found it in one of my traps, then yes, that feels a bit like magic."

Patrok walked into the house and slapped the fish down on the butcher block. "Then call it magic, if you like. To me, it's just lunch." He picked up the filleting knife, considered it with a frown, and sharpened it on the stone before neatly gutting the fish.

The knife had been perfectly sharp, Timeth thought with a ping of resentment. He took pains to keep it that way. Patrok need not have found fault with it—it was like he was trying to show his superiority.

Timeth swallowed the rather unkind thought at the appearance of the succulent, crisped meal, but there were many such instances as the brothers learned to coexist. They would go out to the garden, and Timeth would pull up a spindly turnip while Patrok pulled up one the size of a cat's head. Timeth would notice that the wood pile was dwindling and make plans to fetch wood the next day, only to awaken to the sound of Patrok splitting logs in one chop with what had to be a battle-axe. Patrok offered to teach him how to use the crossbow, but Patrok's shots always struck the bull's-eye, while Timeth's shots frequently went wide.

Each time it happened, Patrok was smiling, kind, eager to explain things. And each time, Timeth would resent him a little more, because he'd done just fine on his own before his big brother had resurfaced, hadn't he? If not, he wouldn't be alive. Perhaps the Druids did things better, with some sort of secret, invisible magic, but there was nothing wrong with the way Timeth carried on day to day.

As Patrok spun tales of trees the size of mountains and conversing with eagles, Timeth had to actively refrain from rolling his eyes. Instead, his thoughts rode the winds of distrust, and his heart began to turn. Patrok was his brother, but he was strange, and for all his endless words, he never really seemed to say anything real, anything about himself.

One night, Timeth woke with a full bladder to find Patrok missing from his place before the door, his weapons left behind, leaning neatly against the wall. Across the room, the door was noticeably unlocked. The wood was cold against Timeth's hand as he pulled the door open, just enough to see the midnight world beyond. The gibbous moon lit the softly swaying branches and flowers, limning the old stone wall in clear, cold blue. Movement caught Timeth's eye, and he saw Patrok pull open the garden gate and pass beyond. In his hand, he held his twisted staff, and the crystal set in its clutches glowed a sinister shade of green. Patrok silently closed the garden gate, and Timeth lost sight of him. He shut the door and sat on the bed, his mind reeling.

What was Patrok doing? Should Timeth follow him out into the forest?

But no. It was dangerous out there, and if Patrok didn't know it, he'd soon find out. Timeth waited all night, his fingers curled around the fish knife under his pillow, his eyes trained on the unlocked door. He must've fallen asleep at some point, or perhaps he'd dreamt it, because when he woke at dawn, Patrok was back asleep on the floor, snoring.

A hundred times that day he opened his mouth to ask Patrok about the midnight wandering he'd witnessed, and a hundred times his mouth snapped shut. If Patrok was doing something bad—something evil—out in the corrupted woods, then it's not like he was going to tell the truth, anyway.

The next night, Timeth feigned sleep, and he again bore witness as Patrok rose with nimble silence, glanced toward the bed, and left. After counting to ten, Timeth crept to the door and watched him slip through the gate. The next morning, Patrok was asleep on the floor, a brace of hares hanging from the ceiling. Patrok promised to make him a warm hat for the winter. Timeth ate his stew and tried to smile, but inside, he was shriveling up like a snail in salt. Even if he pretended to be a good, caring brother, Patrok was lying to him, or at the very least, doing something he shouldn't.

On the next night, Timeth waited until Patrok was outside, then silently rose from his bed, took up his brother's abandoned crossbow, and followed. Once Patrok was out the gate, Timeth scurried in his wake, following the bobbing green light of that strange, twisted staff, which was surely not the work of the holy Druids. Patrok must've been corrupted, just like the land. The dark must've seeped into him. Timeth had to know for sure.

Oddly, Patrok followed the old, overgrown trail up the hill toward the village, right where he—and their mother before him—had made Timeth promise he would never go. Timeth kept to the trees, darting from shadow to shadow, as he followed. Once Patrok was over the hill, he disappeared, and Timeth hurried to catch up . . .

But then he heard a horrible din—a scream and a growl and a wet, ripping sound—and as he crested the hill, he found something his mind struggled to understand. A great beast, like a shaggy gray wolf standing on two legs, reared up over a man, who cowered in fear. Another figure lay on the ground, sickly still and splattered in blood that shone black in the moonlight.

"No, please!" the cowering man screamed, but the wolf-thing raised its wicked claws and slashed out the man's throat in a great gush of blood. The body fell to the ground by its fellow, and the wolf-thing bent over them, sniffing intently, jaws open.

The first man on the ground—was it Patrok? There was his cloak, lying on the overgrown path, so surely it must be.

His brother, splayed lifeless on the ground. Timeth, alone and forsaken yet again.

Hands shaking, heart yammering, Timeth held up the crossbow, trying to remember everything Patrok had taught him. But he wasn't quite close enough, and so he hurried forward, the crossbow held before him, until he knew he could hit his mark.

Squinting through one eye, he took aim. As if sensing his resolve, the wolf-thing's snout spun toward him, its evil, glowing eyes locking onto his, flying wide as it recognized its peril.

"This is for Patrok," Timeth said, and he released the bolt.

Thwack!

Timeth reeled with the force of the shot, but the beast's surprised squeal told him he'd found his mark. The bolt stuck out of its foul, muscular chest, a black stain spreading through the long gray fur. Whimpering, the monster stumbled and fell to all fours like the wolf it so resembled. Its eyes again met Timeth's, soulful and sad—there was something about that gaze that struck Timeth, though he couldn't place it—as it looked up at the clear sky and loosed a weird, tortured howl that sent the night birds shrieking from the trees.

> **TIMETH REELED WITH THE FORCE OF THE SHOT, BUT THE BEAST'S SURPRISED SQUEAL TOLD HIM HE'D FOUND HIS MARK.**

As Timeth watched, the creature fell to its side on the path and curled up, shrinking into itself. Its fur fell away like wheat under a scythe, revealing smooth alabaster skin traced with blue tattoos. Its snout shrank until its face was no longer so monstrous, and a glowing amulet appeared on its chest.

There in the moonlight lay Patrok, the bolt lodged in his heart.

Timeth ran to his brother and knelt beside him.

"Brother, it was you! But how? What—"

"Druid magic," Patrok whispered. "These thieves were on their way to the cottage. They would've killed you. I told you I would always look out for you."

"You—you—you kept sneaking away at midnight! And you had that strange staff. I thought you were corrupted!" Timeth wailed.

"Only as the wolf could I hunt for you and protect you. I wasn't ready to show you yet." Patrok chuckled, and blood burbled out the side of his mouth. "Didn't want to scare you." Patrok pulled his golden amulet over his head and motioned Timeth near. "Take this to the Druids at Túr Dúlra. They will show you—they will—"

The amulet landed heavy around Timeth's neck as Patrok fell back, his eyes empty.

Timeth stood, his fingers wrapped around the heavy stone, the metal chain still warm from Patrok's body. Looking down, he could see in this man the boy he'd once loved above all else.

But Patrok the man had kept things from him. He could change into this terrifying monster, could rip out a man's throat with one careless slash of his talons. How did Patrok *know* these men were evil, that they were on their way to the cottage? Maybe Patrok took the guise of the wolf to rob unsuspecting travelers. How else could he possess the gold and gem of this very amulet?

A noise in the woods startled Timeth, and he grabbed the crossbow and ran toward the cottage as if being pursued by another wolf-man. He burst through the wooden gate, pounded up to the house, threw himself inside, and locked the door. He was panting as he reloaded the crossbow and stoked the fire. Tonight he would not sleep. The world had shown him exactly what lay beyond the stone wall, and he wanted nothing of it.

The next morning, once dawn was fully established, Timeth opened the door to a confusing sight. The garden sagged, the plants brown and limp. The ground was covered in spent blossoms, the trees skeletal and rattling. He took up the crossbow and scurried along the path toward the village, no longer heeding the cautioning words of his mother and brother. When he crested the hill, he found Patrok's cloak and staff gone, his body nothing but gnawed bones, tangled up with the skeletons of the other two men as if animals had fought over them. He remembered in that moment how his brother's last words had been kind, loving, and understanding, free of blame or anger, just like the Patrok he remembered from his earliest days—patient and noble to the last. The amulet under his shirt glowed warm as if in agreement. It was like a bolt to his own heart, realizing that he'd been wrong.

The darkness had not found Patrok.

Timeth had.

Tears sprang up in Timeth's eyes, for all that he felt his heart must be made of dust. When he looked down the hill at the village, he was shocked to see that it had been totally abandoned and was being subsumed by vines and grasses. There was no hope to be found there.

There was no hope to be found anywhere.

Timeth ran home as fast as his legs would carry him. He slammed the garden gate and shut and locked the door to the house. He was almost out of firewood, and the venison wouldn't last much longer. That night, he sat alone in the scant warmth of a single log, one of the last chopped by Patrok. As he fiddled with the two wooden dogs, one so clumsy and the other so accomplished, he heard something scratching at the door.

He would not go to Túr Dúlra with the amulet and seek out the Druids, as his brother had asked with his dying breath. He would not go anywhere at all.

He would not go outside.

Not ever again.

Yet more dark might seep in.

Beyond That Door There Lies No Light

CATHERYNNE M. VALENTE

ILLUSTRATED BY
KELLI HOOVER

I.

It is raining in the deep of the evening. The kind of freezing, needling rain that pierces even the thickest leather, all the way down to the bone and the soul.

But in the deep of this particular evening, there is a golden glow, nesting at the end of a cobblestone road like a living heart. A tavern, backed up against these old city walls and older hills. Warm, beckoning—and most importantly, dry. The smells swirling out of those round windows pull at anyone with a drop of life left in their veins. Rich meat turning above a banked fire. Earthy ale and sharp spirits to carry pain far away. Sweet rosewater and almond oil, promising company both beautiful and reasonably priced.

A weathered sign swings on rusted iron hooks in the brooding wind. Years have stolen the paint from the wood, but even in the mist the old sigil shines clear. A wax stump on a brass plate with a radiant white orb floating above it.

The Star and Candle.

Not exactly the grandest tavern in Khanduras, but certainly not the seediest.

A woman approaches the door, dragging one foot behind her through half-frozen puddles. She has come from a battle, here or there, near or far—it's all the same these days. She needs the kind of rest even a rich bed cannot provide. A mountain of a person; it's anyone's guess whether she's wearing armor or those great shapes beneath her cloak are only brute, powerful shoulders. Rain runs off the edge of the hood she wears over a hard, scar-slashed face. It hardly matters who 'she is, barbarian or hunter or something more. Tonight she is only a traveler, just one of the many to step through that door, shake off the wet and the gloom, and reach eagerly across the bar for the stuff of life.

Wet, muddy, hungry humanity crowd every

stool, armchair, and table. The din of the supper rush ebbs and flows like an ocean of appetite while a valiant fiddle-and-drum duo tunes up near an enormous stone fireplace. The walls are all bare but for early drunkards leaning against them. The owner never saw the purpose in decorating the place. Anything nice enough to lend an air of sophistication got itself stolen in short order. Heavy iron chandeliers barnacled with centuries of melted wax would do for light. Trenchers of thick stale bread would do for silverware. If you want something pretty to look at while you eat, you have your choice of the massive, cracked, possibly even real khazra skull over the fire or Irmla the serving girl and barmaid and cook, whose cankers act up whenever it rains.

The locals would advise sticking with the khazra. But by the light of the angels, can Irmla cook. She's the reason the Star and Candle has never once run short of coin. A scruffy boy slowly turns a marbled roast the size of a carriage wheel in the hearth as fat drips deliciously down into a wide pan of batter, ready to puff up into the next round of rustic puddings.

The traveler's stomach makes its intentions known. But no one marks her. They have their own appetites to answer. Her rumbling gut is answered by a deep, earnest laugh, the kind of laugh only the truly satisfied belly can muster.

"Come and sit, young lady," booms a merry and vigorous voice. "At my table, there is always room for one more."

The traveler turns and finds the owner of that voice lounging comfortably at the head of a feast not even a king would turn down. Glistening mutton, boiled greens, bowls of buttered mushrooms and honeyed turnips, a steaming eel-pie, and Irmla's glorious golden puddings. The man himself is no less luxurious. He sits in the only cushioned chair the Star and Candle can boast, with a high pronged back and faded velvets. His face is round and red and kind, not very young but still hearty, with a well-trimmed silver-speckled beard, a sturdy shape to him that neither boasts of strength nor betrays weakness, and dancing, mirthful eyes the color of spring leaves. He gestures expansively at the food—and at the circle of empty chairs round his table. Empty, in a tavern so crowded no mortal could tell where the queue for ale ends and the queue for the privy begins. And yet no one moves to take them. No one even comes near. Nor do they steal a single glance toward the meal there, ready to eat, while everyone else waits impatiently for Irmla's attentions.

"I am not young," the traveler answers. Her voice is tired and rough. "Nor much of a lady."

> "I AM NOT YOUNG," THE TRAVELER ANSWERS. HER VOICE IS TIRED AND ROUGH. "NOR MUCH OF A LADY."

"Nevertheless," the stranger beckons her, "sit, sit!"

"I could not take food from your plate, sir," she says, hesitating with her last shred of will. Her belly does not care, but she had a mother, once. She is not completely without manners. "Nor do I have coin for so much. A rind of bread and a pot of gravy will do for the likes of me."

"Nonsense. My dear, I have never in my years

filled a plate only for myself. I am both wealthier and lonelier than I look. Indulge my generous nature." The stranger digs into the bowl of honeyed turnips with a golden spoon. On its long, slender tang, a ruby shaped like the moon glitters bloody in the candlelight. The traveler stares. Where could he have gotten such a thing in a place like this? That spoon alone could buy three such taverns, and he's using it to slop gravy on vegetables.

"Are you a lord?" she asks quietly, her eyes on the ruby.

"Of a kind," he allows. The stranger pauses, holding a steaming spoonful above her empty plate. "I would not share my holdings with a stranger," he coaxes.

"Morzena," she yields at last. "Morzena of Nowhere in Particular, Daughter of Nobody Special."

The lines at the corners of his eyes soften and grow gentle as he serves her. "I'm a fairly clever fellow, Morzena. I can see you are injured, not only in the leg but in the spirit. Are you a veteran of war or a marriage? Or both?"

The traveler has no more resistance left in her. She collapses beside him and eats like a serpent unhinging its jaw. Between mouthfuls she allows: "Towns have walls. Guards. Pikes and alarms. But out there . . . you cannot know what it is like in the open wild. Demons have no fear any longer. Sanctuary is their playground, more than any farmer's home or lord's holdings." She upends a tin bottle of something that smells of birch bark and morning's regret into her throat. "I know each battle is over only when the next one lets fly its first charge. I was married, I think. I seem to remember it. A farm, an orchard, a life. But my husband died long ago."

"Ah," says the stranger with ruddy sympathy. "So did mine. Such a greedy thing is death."

She is too hungry still to do more than mumble condolences.

"Let me share a little secret with you," the rich man whispers with the smallest of conspiratorial smiles. He nods his head toward the great hearth and the musicians furtively gulping plum liquor from their water flasks. "That fiddler is absolutely rubbish. And the drummer? Your sanity may not survive. What would you say to another sort of entertainment?"

Morzena rolls her eyes. Husband or no, her conversations with men always end here sooner or later. "I hear there's a blonde and a brunette upstairs for that," she snaps. "When I grapple with a man, it is he who ends the bout on his back and pierced through."

The stranger pats her hand indulgently. His fingers are cold, even in this warmth. "I would never suggest it. Love is not entertainment. No, I had a quieter game in mind. Less piercing. Not none, but less. I propose to tell you a tale, Morzena of Nowhere. It is a very good one, I promise. And when it is done, if you do not believe it is a true tale, through and through, well, then you must pay me two pennies for an evening's amusement, and we shall each part and go to our destinies. But if you do believe me, then I shall pay you two gold pieces, for there is no price too dear for the truth and a kindly ear willing to hear it."

The traveler pauses, a leg of mutton halfway to her mouth. "But I could simply say I believed you and take your gold, no matter what I thought in my heart. Why not just tell your story if you want to talk? I won't interrupt. I am not . . . a talker."

Her host shrugs. "It's the game of the thing. A

story is only a story, but a game? A game *has a victor and a victim—far more exciting. Which will you be? Which will I? As for your shocking idea of cheating a man you just met out of his riches, well, you may at that. But I am comfortable wagering upon the honor of a knight. I was once one myself. I know the weight of a sword and the weight of a word, and which one lands the harder blow.*" He takes a long sip of hot, bloody-red wine. "*What will it be?*"

She hesitates. The rain outside is so cold. The fire so warm and drowsy. She has a miserable life to return to. Shadows outside these very walls. This seems less an amusement than a waste of time. And yet, the stranger is so pleasant and familiar. And he fed her and gave her a place to rest. Surely that is worth humoring an old man who wants to tell sad tales of the world as it was when he was young enough to believe it would come to any sort of good, as all old men do.

The fiddler begins a ballad. It sounds like a khazra with dysentery.

"*My two or yours,*" she agrees quickly. "*I hope you know how to do right by a story.*" She smiles for the first time, and for a moment, under all her scars, she looks as young as a morning.

The hooded stranger fills her cup again. "*There is no one who knows that trick better than I, girl,*" he answers her gravely.

Morzena drains the cup in one long swallow. The hot wine suffuses through her, warming her all the way down to the bone and the soul.

And then the stranger begins.

II.

There was a moment, in the very barest and most innocent beginning of the world, when there was no war on the face of the land or the sea. Only a moment, barely a blink, and ever after both land and sea have wept and shrieked beneath one blade or another. Or so I have heard.

This tale does not take place in that moment, more's the pity. It would be nicer if it did.

This tale begins before wars had names, when the basic business of living was death. No sin, no clans, just rage against rage, vengeance against vengeance, kin against kin, lover against lover, bodies against the void. Angels, demons, ancients, and long afterward, troublesome, slippery humanity. And these folk, as great as the mountains and as terrible as the night? They have always believed themselves to be the center of everything, the great agents of history, the only truly thinking beings in this world, the only creatures capable of striving, desiring, true choice between cruelty and compassion. The only ones who matter.

But they're wrong. The arrogant bastards.

The trouble is, they're all just too *big*. Even men. They stand so tall they can only see others like them. They miss the small and the strange, the dark and the quiet moving all around them, all the time. In this realm of pain there are not only the celestial, the damned, their lost children, and all their braided history of blood.

There are, everywhere and always, fields and forests and seas and skies teeming with life that knows nothing of us.

There are birds, too, in Khanduras.

There are ravens.

They, too, have a history.

And in the ancient corvid tongue, they call those primal days of nameless slaughter the Long Feast.

Like ancients to men, so were the ravens of old to the crooked crows you will find pecking at dry bones on the crossroads now. When scavengers and tinkers came to glean what last treasures they could from battlefields long cold, they often mistook a raven at her banquet of swollen tongues and unstrung innards for a child in her mourning cloak, hunched over a beloved parent, sobbing with grief.

Until that black shape jerked up its head toward the sun with an eyeball skewered on its beak.

Those were rich days for ravens! The business of life took no effort at all. If there was no brutal meadow full of still-steaming corpses bursting with meat and marrow nearby, one had only to wait an hour or two and the unmistakable sounds of sword against sword would let the whole family know that supper would be ready quite soon.

But it's not only the sweet *twang* of a juicy intestine stretching until it snaps that calls to a raven across mountains and rivers and bare winter woods. That's just food! When the belly is satisfied, the heart next asks its due.

And the heart of a raven hungers not for meat but for *shine*.

It did not matter *what* shone, only that it did, and brilliantly. Coins, gems in the hilts of daggers and scimitars, links of chain mail and shards of plate, medallions hung round headless necks for luck or courage, signet rings on a lord's fat cold thumb, an exposed knob of gleaming white bone, gold thread in the slashed standard of this or that king, silver thread in the shredded tunic of this or that arch-general, a golden lock of a child's hair still clutched in this or that man's shattered, stiffening hand.

The slick of that skewered eyeball.

Ravens yearned for these things the way some men yearn for power. The flicker of some mysterious object as it caught the light of sun or moon pulled them as surely as any chain. They could not resist that chain; they did not want to resist it.

> THEY MISS THE SMALL AND THE STRANGE, THE DARK AND THE QUIET MOVING ALL AROUND THEM, ALL THE TIME.

No bird knew who made them this way. All corvids imagined the world was born from an egg laid by the night sky itself, which, surely, if you could only fly high enough to see it, was the flank of a Great Raven roosting above, keeping her children safe and warm beneath her soft, dark feathers.

And the stars? The stars were no less than the Great Raven's own vast hoard of shine, secreted away over a million years of collecting.

It was a good life. A belly full of blood and a nest full of stolen shine. If any raven today still deigned to speak the common tongue, they would tell you it was wholly unnecessary for history to continue past that point. The Long Feast was the peak of the mountain. Everything else merely dirt.

Into the thick and the red of the Long Feast, two particular ravens were born from a single egg. A rare omen nowadays, but during those fat, joyful centuries, anything possible was frequent. Perhaps they were special, perhaps they were not. Perhaps they were just two ordinary birds no different than their kin. Perhaps they were blessed, perhaps cursed, perhaps chosen for greatness or trapped by circumstance.

They were sisters, and their names were Dolor and Rue.

Even among the swiftest, they flew quicker than lightning. Even among the darkest, sunlight itself died on their backs. Even among the cleverest, their thoughts were nimble and subtle and sharp as shadows moving on water. Any phrase they heard they could repeat flawlessly for years afterward, and in a voice so like the one who spoke it even their own mother would think her little one had come home to her arms. And even among eaters of carrion, their hunger burned.

They were happy. They spent their youth with full bellies, endless songs, and shining nests, which is more than most of us can say for our childhoods.

Then, a day arrived both like and unlike any other day in the life of a raven. The sisters were full-grown. Another nameless war drenched the hills red with blood and snowy with bones. Dolor and Rue answered the dinner bell of blade against shield. So did every bird of their carrion-nation: vultures, crows, rooks, petrels, and sheathbills.

The rest of those brute birds saw nothing but the feast.

The sisters preferred to dine together, and they settled down upon the largest meat-purse they could find: a fat rich man of rank with two arrows pounded through his skull and into the thick grass. He had such pretty blue eyes, eyes that once gleamed with stratagems and feints and now gleamed only as they disappeared into two birds' lightless gullets.

They never did agree on who saw it first. Dolor was pecking at the rib cage to free a path to the sweet tender lungs and spiced heart. She insists the shine showed itself to her first, behind the heart, against the spine, and thus was her private portion, no one else's. Rue had claimed the head, snipping off choice morsels from the earlobes, the nostrils, the tongue, the cheek. She swears the shine broke free when she split the skull-plate and therefore was her special toy, no one else's.

Sisters are sisters, even when they are ravens.

Whichever of them saw it first, they worked together to free that strange, shining, brilliant thing stuck in the corpse of that warlord. Dolor pried his breastbone from the red well of his chest. Rue clawed open his soft stomach, his throat, his little spleen, like a fall acorn.

And finally, there it was. Lying tangled in death, sparkling like fresh water or new silver or a pearl still salty from the sea. But it wasn't water, or silver, or a pearl.

No jewel any raven had ever seized could compare to the shine of a mortal soul.

The sisters decided to take the lord's soul

away with them to feather a new and splendid nest, a nest to make even the Great Raven envious among her million stars. They would be queens among beasts that flew.

It took all their strength to pry it free. Blood and cold bile soaked their plumage, their beaks, their claws. They dripped with humanity and didn't care. The shine had them in its grip. But as it came loose at long last and the birds tried to carry it off, they found they could not. It slipped through their talons. The lord's soul fell back to the wet earth. It stood and looked around at the killing floor that was once a pleasant wood. It looked at the two black-eyed ravens sodden with its own blood, splattered with scraps of its brain and kidneys. Staring at him with naked craving. Terror and panic filled the eyes of the lord's soul.

"Am I damned, then?" he whispered. "Was I so wicked?"

Dolor cawed loudly in the empty air. "How could we know?" She whistled and trilled in the voice of a milkmaid whose last penny she'd once stolen.

"Idiot," Rue clacked her black bill at him.

The lord's soul flared with rage—and then it was gone. It didn't fade away. It didn't run for the river down below the rolling hills. It didn't burst in a flash of holy light or go up in a gout of hellfire. The shining soul stood in a marsh of blood and rain one moment, and the next it did not.

"No!" cawed Dolor.

"Not fair," agreed Rue.

But in their hearts, a new passion burned every other desire to ash.

The ravens took to the world with a terrible keenness. Before, they had feasted mindlessly on easy prey, like any other eater of cold war-rot.

Now, they *hunted*.

Dolor and Rue barely tasted their particular favorite treats anymore: the pancreas hiding behind the viscera like a little sugared nut, the larynx still tasting of battle-cries and fury, the delicate under-lobes of the brain like oysters in the shell of the skull. All they sought was the shine. The soul.

Human souls—poor, stupid, bumbling, *lost* human souls—seemed unable to find their own way. The shine tangled in the muck of their carcasses, stuck between the mortal realm and wherever it was that men went when their bodies failed them.

It was hard, messy work. But a shine like this demanded nothing less. Dolor and Rue pecked away at cages of cartilage, moats of blood, walls of skin and sinew. All the way down to the bone and the soul.

Each and every time, they *knew* this was the soul they could keep, this was the one that couldn't escape them, the shine they'd use to make their nest.

Each and every time, the soul slipped past them, down a path they could neither follow nor see.

And each and every time, the pitiful gleaming spirit looked at the raven-sisters with horror and loathing. Sometimes they tried to run. Sometimes they tried to fight. Sometimes they tried to bargain, offering their lands, their gold, their titles, even their own children if the great bloody black birds would grant them one more second of life. Sometimes they had strange ideas about besting the ravens at games of chess or footraces or wrestling matches, none of which a mortal had a hope of winning against a raven of the old world, even if it would've made a bit of difference.

"Give us your shine," screeched Rue in the voice of a rogue she'd once called a fool while she stole the fingernails right off his hand. Yet another soul tried to swing a silvery insubstantial fist through her breast. "Fool!"

"We are only ravens," crowed Dolor as the shade of a tall and graceful lady fixed the blood-sopping bird with a fearful, defiant gaze. "You are not ours to ferry. Go bargain with a god or punch a demon if you wish. We have other things to do. Unless you want to be a nest."

But the souls always vanished. Some sooner, some later. Some babbling with fear and madness, some with trembling dignity. Some sick with revulsion at the final discovery that what came for men in their hour of need was not their dear departed nan, not the beautiful face of Hope or Justice, not even a dark nothing, but monstrous, towering beasts with black shears for mouths, wearing the guts of the new dead like war medals.

But all of them, always, escaped. Into some place, past some door, through some veil no raven could touch.

Dolor and Rue learned and grew, and so did humans great and small. Ravens jeweled with arterial spray and crowned in ribbons of liver and lung were better than the alternative. Some mortals could pass through this world to the next on their own. But some got caught in the prison of their bodies, unable to go or stay, and these turned on their houses, their cattle, their allies, chasing them with a hunger almost as fierce as a raven's. The bereaved began placing polished coins near the bodies of their beloveds, to lure the birds and draw their attention to this baron or that lady wife behind castle walls among all the throngs of dead and dying in open fields.

Dolor and Rue very much appreciated how easy these poor, silly, weeping fools made their work. But they were still birds of prey, born without pity, and pity is such a hard trick to learn from scratch that most men die before they can even begin.

The sisters lived this way for a long time. Much longer than ravens usually live any way at all. They did not notice the centuries or question why they should be exempt from the attentions of time.

Ravens are supremely arrogant. If they lived forever, that was only as it should be.

III.

After many eras and ages, the Long Feast began its last course, though no creature at the supper table knew it had been served.

And in a village whose name matters not at all, but was called in those days Dalibor, a boy was hard at the work of growing up, and though his name doesn't matter any more than that of his village, he was called Tylo. Tylo, son of Zahzh, a minor knight with one ancient, doddering tenant who on a good day could not even make moss grow. Tylo the Sinister of Dalibor House to the tax collector, Tylo the Fool to his father and his brothers,

Tylo the Little Lord to every cretinous child of the village who punched him flat because he knew his thumb from a cow's teat and they did not.

He was the eldest, but never the favorite. The son and grandson and great-grandson of burly, barrel-chested fighting men, born with their height, their broadness, their strength, but the mind of a dreamer, a planner, and a friend to the small.

When he was but four, his father took him into the little courtyard of his little holdfast. A practice dummy stood among the straw bales and the horses waiting to be shod. It was a silly thing, really, nothing but straw stuffed into stained linens, stuck on a stick and painted with two splotchy eyes and a ghastly dripping smile. Tylo's father commanded him to strike it down with his wooden practice sword. *Pretend it is Lord Artald of Calamus, sitting on his throne of shit on the other side of the mountain. He is your most hated enemy, in this world and the next. Strike him down for your father's honor!*

Tylo blinked at the grinning scarecrow in confusion. He had never met this Lord Artald. Why should he hate someone he'd never seen in his life? Artald might have been nice, nicer than his father, anyhow. A kindly uncle, with a library in his hall instead of an armory.

Zahzh, father of Tylo, sighed with an exasperation that in four years had already become habit. *Fine, you little idiot,* he barked. *Pretend it is Gelfrid the Blacksmith's rump-headed whoreson, that talking gristle who kicks your shins in on market day yet somehow has more friends than you ever will.*

Tylo swung his sword at once, without thinking, a terrible, crashing blow. The head of the dummy flew off the straw bale and rolled across the courtyard. One of the old warhorses snorted in the cold morning, lifted one hoof, smashed the dummy's face into hay, and began to nibble at it.

Tylo burst into tears. The poor scarecrow! It hadn't done anything to him, and he'd decapitated it and fed it to a horse. It had a *face*, and feelings, probably, and Tylo had murdered it. Anything with a face could be kind. Could need love. Could give it. Anything with a face was alive.

Tylo felt sick and miserable. He turned to his father to make it better, to make the world soft and right again, to assure him it was only straw and a serving girl's old apron.

But the knight would not look at his son, not while the little goblin sniveled and cried over a badly made poppet in front of all his men, any more than he would allow a weakling like that to inherit his good name.

Tylo understood in that moment that there was no place for a bookish boy with so much love in him he could not bear to hurt straw. Not here. Not now. Not in the world men like his father built. He grew strong, broad, and thick, not because he wished to, but because no other choice existed for him. Strong or dead. Those were all the fates he could hope to touch.

But Tylo did not find his true strength in scarecrows and swords. He found it in that single ancient, doddering tenant, a widower far too long in years to do anything much for himself.

Tylo went down the dales to that hut of sod-and-board and begged to work the old man's land for him, yes, even with nothing but broken pride and a willing back to spend on it. To repair his house, bake his bread, carry his water from the well, to tend his few animals, rebuild his crumbling stone walls and rehang his stove-in door, anything that needed lifting, carrying, pushing, pulling, bashing, kneading. The tenant's house became rather sweet and sturdy, with a fire always happy in a clean hearth. The old man's chickens gave two eggs each a day, his cow gave milk long past her best years, and when the king came to tour the holdfast, the finest of the royal warhorses wandered off in the night and found the tenant's old plow nag still short enough in the tooth to bear the splendid colt that followed twelve months later.

Tylo the Lucky, he began to be called, though never by his father, who, through hard work and perseverance, forgot his own son's name and felt much lighter in the heart for it.

But no matter how strong Tylo became, there was always one stronger, taller, wider, more furious and dull, more happy to hate lords they'd never seen—and most of them were his own brothers. And so Tylo began to suspect that perhaps there was a third choice. Strong, dead, or very, very clever.

For he *was* clever.

> THE TENANT'S HOUSE BECAME RATHER SWEET AND STURDY, WITH A FIRE ALWAYS HAPPY IN A CLEAN HEARTH.

When the old tenant finally died, his soul needed no help from bird or priest, having been half-unmoored from his broken body for years. Tylo performed his last feat of strength and service, burying him in the rocky ground that fought so hard to keep its carrots meager and its wheat threadbare.

When he turned the last clod of soil onto the grave, Tylo became aware he was being watched. A man his own age leaned against the gnarled yew tree that overhung the hut. Handsome enough, with a slenderness Tylo had never been allowed to keep. But the youth bore the sort of overlarge crooked nose and heavy brows that somehow both prevented true beauty and turned a face from unobjectionable to unforgettable.

"All that by yourself," the young man said. "Aren't you a miracle?"

This quiet, thoughtful figure was the tenant's grand-nephew and only living heir. Tavian, a cleric who could not only read but write and tally numbers as well. He lived and worked in a city far away, a city so grand Tylo could not even picture it in his head. Might as well try to picture time or desire.

The two became fast friends. They filled the hut with firelight and conversation well into the night. They told each other many secrets and no lies. Tylo admitted that while his gentle mother had taught him his letters, there were no books in his father's house, and he had only in all his days read two volumes, and one was a treatise on how to grow bigger potatoes. Tavian then filled their water-carrying, roof-thatching hours recounting the wonderful, labyrinthine plots of every history, ballad, diary, and yes, potato-breeder's guide he'd ever read, and those hours were the happiest of Tylo's life. He loved the tenant's grand-nephew, though he did not quite understand it. And that unforgettable face looked back at him with the same shy, curious, unexpected warmth.

Tavian stayed much longer than he intended in his grand-uncle's house, long enough that the young man began to pay his rents and learn to help cows calve and seeds grow. If Tylo's father remembered his existence, he certainly would not have approved such a low marriage for his eldest son, but by then he was away on campaign with his second-eldest, who hadn't even cried when the healers dragged him out of his mother.

But every happiest hour ends before long.

Zahzh of House Dalibor was cut down in battle against old Artald as the knight always suspected he would be. So too was his second-eldest. When the will was administered and keepsakes distributed among the remaining sons, the new master of the holdfast did not even bring Zahzh's last gift to his brother himself. He sent Gelfrid's pig-hearted brute of a boy to bash down the hut's long-mended door and leave Tylo's inheritance on the just-swept floor.

A bundle of broken straw, ripped linen, and splotchy painted eyes.

The practice scarecrow from so long ago.

Tylo stared at it. He turned it over in his hands. Then he laughed so loud and so long Tavian worried he would never stop.

"You don't understand," Tylo said. "I am *free*. Free of him. All of them. I have no name, no rank, no lineage. What does it matter whom I marry or what child I never sire? We can *go*. We can take the king's bastard stallion and sell him, buy a thousand books, and live a city life full of ink and wine whose grapes we never had to grow." Tylo gripped Tavian's hand tightly. "You are my wealth, my holdfast, my lucky chicken who lays two eggs at once. You are my House now, and your face is our sigil. House Us and House Always. I am yours, if you'll have me, all the way down to the bone and the soul."

And wouldn't this be a lovely story if that was the end? Some stories end with weddings, I'm told.

But not this one.

Lord Artald was emboldened by victory. His forces swept down through the lowlands, flattening forests and hauling any able-bodied soul away at axe-point to serve in his ranks. He really wasn't kindly or nice in the end. And in the end, Tylo *did* hate him. Not for being an enemy of Dalibor or killing his kin but for proving his father right about anything at all.

Tylo the Lucky became a fighter after all. Unwilling, unhappy, unenthusiastic, but a fighter nonetheless. So was Tavian, briefly, before Artald realized an educated man was much more useful in the strategist's tent among the mages and monks than getting his writing hand hacked off in a half-frozen swamp. That hungry lord in velvet and silver seemed always to know precisely when his favorite tactician had finally set upon that very night to escape—but no one can be vigilant forever, and as soon as Artald let himself indulge in a little extra wine, a little extra meat, his broad-backed knight and his indentured mind slipped out of the command tents and into the safety of shadows and the wild.

They saw the children on the edge of the camp. Filthy, ragged, wounded. War orphans bound to serve their lord's cause.

Tavian begged with his eyes: *Keep going, I cannot bear another day here.*

Tylo answered with his gaze: *Do not stop. Pity will be the end of us if we let it.*

They went straight to the poor beasts and cut their bonds, a boy and a girl, barely older than Tylo had been on that terrible day with the grinning scarecrow in the courtyard. So terrified and hungry they couldn't find the spit to speak, but clung to the kind men as they carried them out of camp and into the mountains. To them, anyone who didn't put a new bruise next to the others was all the kindness in the world.

Aellin and Frix. Fear had struck their family names from memory. Seized in a raid and passed from camp to camp. Little fingers are useful for so many tasks. Aellin mended tunics; Frix fletched arrows; both remembering less and less that once such chores had been only games with dolls and wooden soldiers. Most days whoever beat them assumed someone else had fed them. Most days, she or he or both tried to die off the edge of a ravine or the point of a knife, and failed.

"Well, that is all over now," said Tylo when the little gang was well past catching, safe among great moonless trees and boulders higher than cathedrals. "I cannot promise much, but I can promise that."

And thus, before they even crossed out of Calamus territory, Tylo and Tavian were a family. Who knew well how to build a little nameless sod-and-board hut, capture a wild calf or boarlet and tame it beside whatever game birds the open meadows yielded up, plant seed, trade at market, and fill the nights with something other than darkness—laughter and stories and songs and candlelight, and wonder that the world might make room for such a perfect little life inside its grief.

Aellin was determined to be a knight like her father, but a knight for goodness and love, to protect and not to harm. Frix showed a fearsome talent for numbers even Tavian could scarcely believe.

They lived and grew.

Tylo and Tavian and their children lived that way for a long while. And in certain lights, at certain times of day, when the breeze smelled for a fleeting moment of apples rather than severed bowels and burning bone, despite it all, despite waking screaming in the night trying to outrun memory, despite knowing that dreamed-of house in the city with all its books was far beyond their grasp now . . . they were happy.

Tylo the Lucky returned from the hunt that day with two partridges on his belt. Proud to be bringing home such a feast. Missing his babies, missing his beloved, spring mist cold and clammy on the back of his neck.

But the raiding party had already come and gone. It didn't matter whose sigil they bore; Tylo didn't know and never would. All he saw was his sweet little cottage barely standing, fire and axes and the merriment of the sort that men like his father and brothers loved to make.

Tavian lay by the hearth, slumped over Aellin and Frix. At first, Tylo thought all of them struck through the back with great blades thicker than the babies' arms. Pierced straight through their dear, fragile hearts, all the way down to the bone and the soul.

But after a long, long while, Tavian moved in the ember-light.

When he stood, his chest looked like his own heart had been hacked out. But it was not his blood. It was Aellin and Frix's, dark and thick and still steaming, still hot.

Tylo saw and heard nothing more.

When he came to himself again, it was deep night, Tavian was gone, and he suspected not all the destruction of their perfect little house was the work of the raiders.

Certainly those brutal marauders had not been the ones to leave two gleaming, polished coins beside the ruination of his family, shining in the weak light of a few last embers amid the darkness. Certainly they were not the ones crouched between the children's beds, waiting, seething. Hunting. That was him. Or at least, what he had become. A beast of grief, blind and without memory.

They came just before dawn. Two enormous shapes in the shattered doorframe. Inhuman. Unreal. Black turned blacker with old blood.

"Look, sister," cawed one, jerking her razor-beak toward Tylo's cold, glass-eyed children. "One for each of us."

Tylo the Lucky stood with utter calm, strode across the ruined floor of his life, raised his old war sword, and sliced the ravens' heads off their ancient bodies in one awful blow.

The knight woke before the first light. He broke the ice on his washbasin and made himself presentable. He left his little hut and went out to the barn where they kept their chickens and one pheasant with his brilliant tail warm and dry from the many snows of that country. Aellin had loved that bird. Whenever he dropped a tail feather, she wore it in her hair all day pretending to be a highborn lady. He opened the gate and sat on the still-frozen ground before a massive silver cage.

"Bring them back," he said quietly.

Dolor and Rue, perfectly whole and healthy, hissed at him out of their inky gullets.

"Where did you get this cage?" Dolor screeched. "You are a poor man—anyone can see it. You have no business with so much shine."

"My beloved has read every book worth reading. He taught me to summon what I need. Do not try to pick the lock—it is well made." Tylo ran his hands along his sword, which lay balanced across his knees. Where had Tavian gone? Why would he run from Tylo, now, after all this? But he would return. Of course he would.

"Bring them back," he repeated.

"Idiot," barked Rue. "We can't."

"You are Death. Bring them back, or I will take your heads again. And again, and again, every morning and night, as long as it takes. Bring them back."

"We are not *Death*. We only help men on

their way *to* Death. We are ravens. Birds. We come for the shine. We have no power to bring anyone back, we do not even know where they *go*," Dolor insisted, bristling every feather in rage. *No one* confined them. Not *ever*.

"You *are* Death. If you were not, you would not have heads on your shoulders right now. You resurrected with the dawn. No other bird can do this."

Rue spread her great wings. "The world is a strange place. I cannot explain it any more than you can explain your toenails growing after you cut them. We cannot do what you ask."

Tylo ran his finger along the hilt of his sword. "This isn't right. Or fair. My children suffered enough for fifty lifetimes. They did not deserve this end. You are right: I cannot explain everything in this world. I do not know much, but I am very clever. And I can keep you here as long as I like. Those whose souls you would have carried will not move on. People will suffer. Until you do right by me and make my family whole again. I can wait. They cannot."

"So you will pay your family's ransom through evil? By cursing others to suffer?" Dolor gripped the cage with her talons. "It's not that I *care*, it's just that I'm curious."

Tylo shrugged. He didn't care. Not anymore.

"Bring them back," he said evenly. "And there will be no suffering at all. If a curse settles upon this land, it is you who sent it, not I." He paused. "Stop being so stubborn."

"No matter how many of you think you have found the perfect scheme to catch us, it will always fail because we have no power over life and death," Rue spat. "We are only the messengers. *Fool!*"

"All right," Tylo relented at last.

Then he stood calmly, strode across the chicken pen, opened one side of the beautiful cage, lifted his old war sword, and sliced their heads off again.

IV.

And so, every morning, Tylo the Lucky went to feed his birds, said three simple words, listened to the worst words any raven knows hurled down upon him, and cut their heads off once more before returning to boil the eggs he'd collected for breakfast.

Bring them back.

All the while, the nameless wars curdled, even in victory, even in triumph.

Those whose souls could go forth and find their way to whatever followed life in this vale of blood alone did. The rest, their spirits tangled in their bodies like fish in a net of sinew, dragged that flesh behind them, into villages, into castles, into citadels, unseeing, unfeeling, unyielding. Hungry for life. Hungry for heat. And every drop of their congealed blood, every sliver of bone, every rotting organ in unending, individual, shrieking pain.

After a time, Tavian did return. With hollow, uncertain eyes and a flinch in his footsteps. They didn't speak of it; they couldn't. The words to make all things right again had spilled away into the hungry earth, just the same as that easy city wine they'd never drunk together. Just the same as the blood of their sweet babies, buried now above the river where they could see the light on the water.

He could have let them go then. Tylo knew

that. He knew that summoning them and imprisoning them might be forgivable, in a certain light, with a certain understanding of pain. He also knew Tavian would think it a dreadful sin, because it was, it simply *was*, there was no logic that could make Tylo a good man again. Not if he kept the ravens now, with his beloved returned to him and life churning on everywhere.

But Tylo couldn't let the *idea* go. That it could happen. That they would, finally, someday, in the end, relent and Aellin and Frix would come through the old wooden door full of laughter and pheasant feathers and flapping silver fish on a line, fish from the river that flowed past their graves. So he simply asked Tavian to let him look after the animals and save his strength for better things, leave the silly old barn alone, it's about to fall to pieces anyhow, let only one of us risk a falling rafter to the spine.

And Tavian was tired, and frightened, and ate his grief for every meal, with double helpings on holy days.

One night he looked up at Tylo and whispered:

"When I see your face in the firelight, all I can see is how it twisted that night, how the man I know vanished, and was replaced with pain as pure as an element. How you took your fists to our house. How you screamed."

"I am so sorry," Tylo said softly.

"And when I see your face in the daylight, all I see are Aellin and Frix, how she lifted one eyebrow when she was about to give me a piece of her mind, just like you do. His little half-grin when he knew a secret, just like yours. My only peace is in darkness, when I see nothing."

Tylo didn't say anything then, soft or hard. There are agonies no words can speak to. There are some moments that end a human heart. The human goes on, for years, decades, even, but some part of their heart is always living in those terrible hours, and cannot find any door in the dark that opens outward.

It will all be forgiven when the ravens bring them back, he thought. *He will see me when he looks at my face again. Just me, as I was on the day we met, ready to build reality with my bare hands if it meant a life as one. He'll see. It will all be as it was.*

> TAVIAN WAS TIRED, AND FRIGHTENED, AND ATE HIS GRIEF FOR EVERY MEAL, WITH DOUBLE HELPINGS ON HOLY DAYS.

But the next morning Tavian was gone. He'd gone to bury his misery in the strategist's tent. To help stave off the scourge of half-corpses lurching over the land. Any enemy of Lord Artald would have a ready mind to make each blow count for ten.

Tylo stared down the valley and over the river, into the woods beyond and the disputed territories where he'd once been young, once fought, once dreamed of better. He stared for a long time, letting the spring rain drench him, down to the bone and the soul.

Then he went back into the barn with the silver cage.

Bring them back.

And in this manner, he grew old. Silver came to his hair and his beard, weakness came to his limbs, and mist and misery came to his mind. But still each morning he did the most terrible business of his farm, and the ravens' heads rolled through the dawns between milking the cows and checking the cider barrels. He began to talk to the ravens before the inevitable deed; their talks stretched longer and longer as the seasons came and went. Longest in the autumn, Death's natural season. Dolor and Rue came to know him, and he came to know them.

"Perhaps," Dolor suggested to her sister in the late endless hours before morning, "if he comes to like us well enough, he will just . . . free us."

Rue nuzzled her sister with her dark head. "Idiot," she said fondly.

And no matter what they spoke of, what secrets were shared between the three, the conversation always ended with a terrible blow and a spray of red on the earth.

After some years, Tylo added another word to his daily prayer. And then three more.

Bring them back.
Aellin. Frix.
Tavian.
Please.
I'm so sorry.

And then it came to pass that one morning, when all the old hens still slept, Tylo's dark, hunched shape shuffled out from his hut, into the pen, past the elderly grandson of that splendid pheasant Aellin had loved so.

The old bird had dropped a long, fiery-colored tail-feather.

Tylo plucked it from the gray earth and put it in his hair.

The ravens looked at him from behind their silver prison with resignation.

"Just do it and get it over with. I've no patience with dread today," Dolor sighed.

Rue fixed her lovely onyx eyes on the old man as he opened the door. "Please believe me," she whispered. "We would do it if we could."

Tylo thought he was too old for tears. That they had all dried up long ago like rain on sand. But he wept as he lifted his war sword for the ten thousandth time. The effort was terrible. His joints howled, and his breath scraped his chest bare as it left him. The sword swung high above his head, high enough to catch the sun and shine like hope. Like the possibility of change.

And standing thus, in the frigid light, Tylo's heart shuddered and stopped. His body sank slowly to the dusty, hen-scratched ground.

"Poor, stupid bastard," Dolor said sadly, shaking her head.

Rue hopped nimbly out of the cage and shivered, feeling her claws on real dirt for the first time in so long. "I have been thinking," she said. "Just the last decade or two. That they are all poor, stupid bastards. But it is not so stupid to *try*. To hope something broken can be fixed." She cawed in the fog. "It can't, of course. But they would not be men if they did not try. He tried a lot. I liked him for that, at least."

Then she bent her head like a holy woman and ripped Tylo's chest open in a glut of scarlet.

It wasn't hard work, not for two hungry ravens and an old man's paper skin. The shine was there. They would find it. Under his ribs or behind his lungs, stuck between his stomach and his spine. Dolor and Rue had spent a lifetime with Tylo. They would take him the rest of the way home.

There it was. Sparkling in all the wet ruin of his corpse. The secret glittering core of Tylo of Dalibor, the child who could not even bear to hurt straw.

Just like all the others, his spirit melted out of their beaks like summer butter and he stood before them. Smiling, eager, at ease. And so young. In the fullness of his strength.

"I am, you know," his soul said. "So sorry. Tylo the Fool, children called me once. I suppose they were right in the end."

"Yes," agreed Dolor.

"Yes," agreed Rue.

"I feel the pull of it. The path out, and away," Tylo said softly. His soul looked down the tree line, toward the plains and the great cities. "How can I face them? They will know what I have done."

"Good luck," chirped Dolor. "I hear a battle in the east, and I mean to *feast*."

"Look on the bright side," Rue cawed. "Maybe there is nothing at all after death and you'll just cease to exist without ever seeing your family again!"

The ravens flew away down over the moors and the foothills, down toward the clanging dinner bells of sword against bone, wheeling and whirling in the sky with the rushing joy of freedom.

But when they alighted on the aftermath of a river battle, Tylo's soul stood amongst the banquet, waiting for them.

He watched as they ate. He watched as they worried the shine free of the flesh. He watched as souls quailed and shook and screamed in terror at the vision of two hulking ravens dripping with gore that greeted them instead of the soft, warm place their nans had promised. He watched the souls flee without soothing, without softness, without succor.

"Go away," Rue snapped finally. "Haven't you done enough?"

"I don't think I have," Tylo whispered.

"Don't you have a fathomless void of mystery calling to you?" sang Dolor.

"I do," the old knight admitted. "But it is only a call. I can ignore it. If I choose."

"Don't," advised Rue, gnawing on somebody's ear.

Tylo the Lucky put a gentle hand out to the ravens of death. "Anything with a face is alive," he murmured, almost to himself. "Anything with a face can be kind. Let me be your face. Let me stand in your stead so that the first thing a soul sees is not the carrion birds who came to eat her. Let me take the challenges of fools like me, to bargain, to fight, to capture, to trick. They can never harm me as I could harm you. If you are the truth, let me become the story. Let me ... let me do penance. Let me become worthy again in the eyes of my dead children. When I have toiled enough to right my books, then I will go to them. But I do not think that will be soon." The ravens did not answer. Tylo knelt. "I can resist the call. Every day. To do our good work. To make Death kind. To save the scarecrow in the courtyard from having to look my father's horse in the teeth. I will be your straw dummy, wear your face over my emptiness. To take the blows meant for you. To smile . . . whilst you help us free of ourselves." His silvery hands twisted one another. "And perhaps, one day, someone in particular will approach the door at the end of life. And perhaps I could be the one on the other side, then."

"We have . . . been lonely. From time to time," Dolor admitted at last. "It hurts when they scream in such fear. We cannot help how we look. We are *trying*. Trying to be kind. Trying to help. Trying to be useful to the world. But they call us such names."

"And some of them cut our heads off," cawed Rue. "A lot."

"Well," said Tylo of Dalibor, Tylo the Fool, "that is all over now. I cannot promise much. But I can promise that."

Rue looked fondly upon the face of Death.

"You silly *idiot*," she said warmly, and enveloped him in an infinite expanse of black feathers, all the way down to the bone and the soul.

V.

"*Well?*" *says the stranger.*

Morzena has finished the turnips, the eel pie, the mutton leg, the carrots and the mushrooms. Her brain is beginning to get fuzzy with warmth and wine.

"*Well what?*" *she says with a small burp, well-concealed.*

"*That is my tale. Do you believe it? Two pennies if you do not, two gold coins if you do, and remember our bargain.*"

The traveler wants to lie. There are two gold pieces in it for her if she lies. Because of course it is absurd. Lord Death isn't two ravens unstuck from the tar of history. Lord Death is . . . Lord Death. It is silly and off-putting and while children dying is always a sad thing, she didn't know them. Most likely, they'd never lived. It is in her best interest to lie. Two gold pieces could keep her brain fuzzy for quite some time. Morzena opens her mouth to lie.

"*What happened to Tavian?*"

The stranger's half-smile becomes a full one. "He died an old and very rich man. When Artald finally got himself bludgeoned to death on the battlefield, he retired. He started a winery. I believe Irmla serves his claret even today. He spent his years among the grapes, and took in anyone who was lost, but especially children who had no one but hunger to tuck them in at night. Everyone loved him for miles around. And when he died," *the stranger's voice catches,* "*when he died, a great tall man in a dark cloak with a bird on each shoulder came for him. A great tall man who had known for some time that in this way and in this guise, he would one day find his love again. Death comes for all of us, after all. But Death comes for some of us with a grave face, and for some of us with such joy it would shatter the sun.*

Lord Death held his beloved's face in his hands, and kissed him all over his funny old forehead with terribly cold lips, and told him everything, all of it, from the cage up to that very moment, all the souls he had seen, all the stories he had learned, more stories from more souls than any vault of books could contain.

'*All that by yourself?*' *coughs Tavian as the light in him dims. 'Aren't you a miracle?*'

'*Do you forgive me?*'

'What in the world are you on about, of course I forgive you. Being ninety years old is a wonderful cure for the disease of judging others. We all tried. We tried very hard. I forgive you forever. House Us.'

'And House Always. My holdfast.'

It is said Lord Death wept once in all his long duty, only once, when the moon rose and Tavian did not."

The stranger pats her hand and pushes her to finish the last bites of stew-soaked bread.

His face catches her. Something in the laugh lines and ruddy cheeks, the angle of his beard and the way he sits so comfortably in that broken throne of a chair. He has been kind to her. He has fed her and given her a place to sit when there was none.

"No," she tells the truth at last. "I do not believe it. It's only a story. The kind drunkards always tell in taverns. Ridiculous, impossible, a little blasphemous—but entertaining enough. You are an excellent storyteller." She hands him two tarnished pennies.

The stranger smiles sadly, pocketing them. "This will be much harder then."

He passes two new-minted coins across the beaten table toward her. They have to be new—they shine so. "Although you do not yet believe me, take my gold coins anyway. You need them more than I."

Morzena stares at them. The firelight on their surfaces dances.

"I walked so far," she whispers. She cannot seem to swallow, suddenly. "From the battlefield. Everyone else was killed. I came so far. All the way to the town. All the way here."

"Yes," the stranger says. "But no. Not really. Not in the end."

"I don't believe you."

"You will. And then the four of us will all take a long walk together, along whatever route brings you joy and memories, all the way out of the world. I found him, and I found you. As I find all who need me. But some . . . more than others. Who are lost. Who have lost. Who are loved. Who have loved," the stranger says, and his voice is so full of love and acceptance. It almost sounds like her husband's voice. The way ravens can mimic men. The stranger cradles her face in his hands, which seems suddenly much older and thinner than they did when she first met him.

He refills her cup.

"Drink up. And savor it. Make it last. It won't be long now, my dear. They always come for the shine."

About the Authors

INTRODUCTION

JUSTIN PARKER

Justin is a longtime employee of Blizzard Entertainment and a fan of the Diablo franchise for a little bit longer. In this time he has not fallen to the corruption of the Lord of Terror—yet.

SHORT STORIES

MATTHEW J. KIRBY

Matthew is the critically acclaimed author of more than a dozen novels for teens and young readers, including *The Clockwork Three*, *Icefall*, *A Taste for Monsters*, and the Assassin's Creed series *Last Descendants*, as well as *Geirmund's Saga*, an original story connected to the world of the Assassin's Creed game *Valhalla*. He has won several awards, including the Edgar Award and a PEN Center USA Award, and his books have been selected by the Junior Library Guild and the American Library Association for their lists of best fiction for young adults. He and his family currently live in Idaho.

TAMSYN MUIR

Tamsyn is the bestselling author of the Locked Tomb series. Her fiction has won the Locus Award and the Crawford Award and has been nominated for the Hugo Award, the Nebula Award, the Shirley Jackson Award, the World Fantasy Award, the Dragon Award, and the Eugie Foster Memorial Award. A Kiwi, she has spent most of her life in Howick, New Zealand, with time living in Waiuku and central Wellington. She currently lives and works in Oxford, in the United Kingdom.

COURTNEY ALAMEDA

Courtney is a horror novelist and comic book writer. Born and raised in the San Francisco Bay Area, she now resides in the northwestern United States with her husband, one Welsh corgi, two cats, three library rooms, and whatever monsters lurk in the rural darkness around her home.

ADAM FOSHKO

Adam is an acclaimed screenwriter, story director, and narrative designer. Having developed and written on the long-running Skylanders, Call of Duty, Destiny, James Bond, and Medal of Honor franchises, as well as with MGM, Paramount, DreamWorks, and HBO, he now works with Blizzard in the Story and Franchise Department on *Diablo*, *Overwatch*, and others. He continues to write and develop for film, television, and games.

BARRY LYGA

Barry has been gaming since the age of ten, when his father foolishly bought an Atari 2600 and set it up in the basement. He started reading short story collections around the same time, so this was fated. Called a "YA rebel-author" by *Kirkus Reviews*, Barry has published twenty-five novels in various genres in his fourteen-year career, including the *New York Times* bestselling *I Hunt Killers* and the origin of the Marvel Cinematic Universe's Thanos in *Thanos: Titan Consumed*. He lives on the outskirts of New York City with two children who are smarter than he is and his wife, the novelist Morgan Baden.

BRIAN EVENSON

Brian is the author of more than a dozen books of fiction, most recently the story collection *The Glassy, Burning Floor of Hell*. His collection *Song for the Unraveling of the World* won the Shirley Jackson Award and the World Fantasy Award and was a finalist for the *Los Angeles Times'* Ray Bradbury Prize. Other prizes include the 2009 American Library Association's RUSA award for *Last Days* and the International Horror Guild Award for *The Wavering Knife*. He is the recipient of three O. Henry Prizes, a National Endowment for the Arts Fellowship, and a Guggenheim Fellowship. His work has been translated into more than a dozen languages. He lives in Los Angeles and teaches in the Critical Studies Program at CalArts.

DELILAH S. DAWSON

Delilah is the author of the *New York Times* bestseller *Star Wars: Phasma* and *Star Wars Galaxy's Edge: Black Spire*, *The Violence*, *Mine*, *Camp Scare*, the Minecraft: Mob Squad series, the Hit series, the Blud series, the Tales of Pell series (with Kevin Hearne), and the Shadow series (written as Lila Bowen), as well as the creator-owned comics *Ladycastle*, *Sparrowhawk*, and *Star Pig*, plus comics in the worlds of *Firefly*, *Star Wars*, *The X-Files*, *Adventure Time*, *Rick and Morty*, *Marvel Action: Spider-Man*, Disney's *Descendants*, *Labyrinth*, and more. Find her online at delilahsdawson.com.

CATHERYNNE M. VALENTE

Catherynne is a *New York Times* and *USA Today* bestselling author of forty books of fantasy and science fiction, including *Space Opera*, the *Fairyland* series, *Deathless*, and *The Orphan's Tales*. She lives on a small island off the coast of Maine with her partner and child.

WRITERS

Introduction	Justin Parker
The Gospel of Death	Matthew J. Kirby
The Rose of Khanduras	Tamsyn Muir
A Collar of Thorns	Courtney Alameda
The Caravan	Adam Foshko
A Whiff of Salt	Barry Lyga
The Tomb of Tal Rasha	Brian Evenson
When the Dark Seeps In	Delilah S. Dawson
Beyond That Door There Lies No Light	Catherynne M. Valente

ILLUSTRATORS

Borders and Cover Illustration	Joseph Lacroix
The Gospel of Death	Stanton Feng
The Rose of Khanduras	Josh Tallman
A Collar of Thorns	Stanton Feng
The Caravan	Zoltan Boros
A Whiff of Salt	Joseph Lacroix
The Tomb of Tal Rasha	Josh Tallman
When the Dark Seeps In	Zoltan Boros
Beyond That Door There Lies No Light	Kelli Hoover

BLIZZARD ENTERTAINMENT

Diablo: Tales from the Horadric Library

ISBN: 9781803361659

Published by Titan Books, London, in 2022.

Published by arrangement with
Blizzard Entertainment, Inc., Irvine, California.

© 2022 Blizzard Entertainment, Inc. Blizzard and the Blizzard Entertainment logo
are trademarks or registered trademarks of Blizzard Entertainment, Inc.
in the U.S. or other countries.

No part of this publication may be reproduced, stored in a retrieval system, or transmitted, in any form or by any means without the prior written permission of the publisher, nor be otherwise circulated in any form of binding or cover other than that in which it is published and without a similar condition being imposed on the subsequent purchaser.

2 4 6 8 10 9 7 5 3 1

TITAN BOOKS

A division of Titan Publishing Group Ltd
144 Southwark Street
London SE1 0UP

www.titanbooks.com

Find us on Facebook: www.facebook.com/titanbooks

Follow us on Twitter: @TitanBooks

A CIP catalogue record for this title is available
from the British Library.

Printed in China